Also by Ron Savage

Novels
Scar Keeper
Sharing Atmosphere
Cheap Meat
The Dreaming Field
Saving Face
Nasty Creatures
Silence of My Father
The Doll Harvest
Devious Pilgrims

Collections
Loving You the Way I Do
What We Do for Love

Novelettes
River of the Pink Dolphin

VOYEUR IN TANGIER

RON SAVAGE

FOMITE
BURLINGTON, VT

ISBN-978-1-944388-12-6
Library of Congress Control Number: 2017941179

Author Photo:
Cover Art
"Vulture" © Eben Markowski

To Janny, always

I would liken you
To a night without stars
Were it not for your eyes.
I would liken you
To sleep without dreams
Were it not for your songs.

-- Langston Hughes

ONE

PARIS TO TANGIER
SEPTEMBER 1974

THE MAN SEATED NEXT TO ME says he can see the coast of Spain and beyond that, the North Atlantic. He is tan-skinned and overweight and his cologne is too strong for close company. What can you do with a man who must either breathe loudly or talk? I nod and smile without looking up from my book. I have never cared for airplanes. It's a mystery why we enjoy looking at the earth from so high off the ground.

Both my parents insisted I take this trip. "Go get your life back, Liora," one or the other has said over the years – or versions of it. They believe life is a thing someone can steal from you the way a burglar will grab a fur coat or silverware. I think they are on to something; this stealing business is real. But their talk may have more to do with old ghosts than with me and I'm not sure I want those old ghosts to leave anytime soon.

MY BEST INTEREST was not considered, let me be honest. I know things in the past should be left in the past but that is easier for the innocent than the guilty. Tell me what a person ought to do if that person's parents offered her up to save themselves? Tell me that, please. Suppose you were a thirteen-year-old girl and your caring and delightful parents did that to you. "All of us have to sacrifice one way or the other," they'd say – or versions of it. Wouldn't a normal child think, Wait a minute. Where is the protection? Where is the love? What's wrong with you people?

This occurred thirty years ago, May 1944, when the Nazis had imprisoned us in Theresienstadt. My family and I were living in Prague. Before Theresienstadt, we kept our house locked and our lights off and we did not answer the knocks on the door without asking, "*Kdo je tam*?" Who's there? Buses and trucks rolled through our neighborhoods and shook the cups and saucers on our dinner tables.

Soldiers walked the streets, talking and laughing. We also heard rifle shots but that was usually at night and not too often.

No one escaped the war. The war brought us an untamable fear and the children were scared and their parents were scared and we all tried to figure the angles and how to sneak into another day.

I LOVE MY mother and my father but my love is muddled by their old decisions and my memories of them when I was a thirteen-year-old. And that love is far from perfect. I remember a dear friend saying to me, "Yesterday looks different in the present." This is a woman who has not been wrong since I've known her and that friendship is getting close to seventeen years now. Reba, that's her name, my Peruvian friend, Miss Reba. I confess I do think about my parents and wonder how many years do I want to hold on to bad feelings?

I should have a more forgiving heart.

Last week President Ford pardoned Nixon. Everybody I know is furious. Many people feel Nixon's a criminal. Once again burglars have taken other people's things. Burglars have gone into places that were private and swiped the silverware.

I teach undergraduate anthropology at The

College of William and Mary and my students and my faculty friends are stunned by the pardon. They're hurt and angry and want revenge. To them, Richard Nixon is Shylock and Judas. Nixon is sweat and greasy hair and a five o'clock shadow. He has become the car dealer ready to sell you a clunker.

Would you buy a used car from this man?

Students and faculty walk the halls with their shoulders hunched and their hands above their heads, forefingers and middle fingers shaping a V. "I am not a crook!" they say to each other and laugh. They are all outraged but amused. It's fun. It's a joke. It's treachery and sadness. It's sweet Pat Nixon having a cocktail or two in her lovely cloth coat while her hubby and Henry Kissinger are on their knees in the oval office with an impromptu prayer. And what *was* that prayer? That's what I'd like to know. Did Nixon understand that his last prayer in the Whitehouse was done not with Billy Graham but holding hands with the king of the Harvard Jews?

It's so American, so crazy and wonderful.

Satisfaction and revenge have become the country's drugs of choice. But Jerry Ford wants none of it. He does not want the stigma of Nixon-in-chains wandering the Whitehouse.

THE WATERGATE BURGLARS brought out different feelings for me. I thought about my parents saying, "Go get your life back, Liora." I had my own thief and my own missing silverware. Colonel K.P. Kohler, the officer in charge of Theresienstadt, this was my thief, my burglar. I used to call him Colonel Smiley – not to his face, of course. The man's smile was his only expression and he hid himself in that smile.

My fantasies about finding the Colonel have changed over the years. When I was younger I wanted to find him and give him a speech and shoot him. My speech would be about killing Jews and how true justice will always win out against hideous sociopathic Nazis.

Then *Boom*! Right between the eyes.

Sixteen years ago, my plan changed. Miss Reba had said, "What you want is your life back. Go see how yesterday looks different in the present."

I did not know where to go to get my life back. I had wanted to sit down with the Colonel after all these years and just talk to him. That was my new plan, Reba's plan. I would go see how time and circumstance punishes us all. But Colonel Kohler could've been anywhere—Brazil, Argentina, South America, anywhere. Over the years my father and I hired many people to help me find this man. Then we hired Leon Nauman. And last week Leon called me and said, "I'll meet you in Tangier on the 17th."

"I can't just go to Tangier."

"Who says?"

THE OVERWEIGHT MAN next to me is snoring, his mouth open, his head against the backrest. This snoring stops and starts and has no true rhythm. Now our plane banks to the left and I look at the windows across the aisle and see the blue and slate color of the Mediterranean and, further on, the North African shoulder that is Morocco.

I hate flying but I love where flying takes me.

Each summer I leave university life and travel to South America and the Amazon. My research includes Peru, the Amazonas, Loreto, Acre, Brazil, and the Eastern Andean regions of Ecuador. What I have been studying over the years is Shamanic healing and their use of pharmaceuticals. More than a hundred and twenty prescription drugs come from plants and twenty-five percent of all our drugs come from the Amazon. There are 3,000 plants in the rainforest that are used just to fight cancer.

Most curanderas in the area are seventy years old or older. And the younger women are not becoming curanderas. The young have become far too educated and too worldly and all they want to do is leave the jungle. They do not care about their history or the old women who cure illnesses. What is worse, the curanderas don't keep records of what they do and how they do it. Think about that, think about the tremendous loss of knowledge. We aren't talking about quaint cultural rituals here. We are talking about the ways humans have of healing one another. And the healers are dying. They die every day.

I have been interviewing these old women for years, recording what they have done and what they are doing now. This is my life's work.

How do you approach an illness? I want to know. *Is a spiritual issue different than a physical issue? And if so, how? What medicines do you use and how do you go about making them?*

There are many, many questions. And I feel the pressure of time.

SINCE BEGINNING MY trip, I have been thinking a lot about Miss Reba. She is one of the old ones. I believe she was the person who gave me the courage to step back in time and look at myself and what happened to me and my family. I could feel her presence at the beginning of this trip. I can feel her presence now.

I first met Miss Reba in the small town of Pisac, near the Urubamba River. This was the Spring of 1958, I think. I had just started the year of field work I needed for my dissertation in cultural anthropology at Southern Illinois. I chose the *Ayahuasqueros* as my specialty, the Peruvian curanderas who make a hallucinogenic mixture called *ayahuasca*. The ingredients are the *Banisteriopsis* vine and the leaves of *Psychotria viridis* and these are boiled for several hours and used by the *Ayahuasqueros* for both physical and psychic healing.

That morning the Sacred Valley had wet grass and slick gray rock. The sky was gray and the clouds came and went. The Inca ruins start at the tops of the mountains and curve along the slopes. These ruins slow the wind and keep the winter ice until late in the Spring. What is left of the buildings are shaved and perfectly fitted stones that do not need mortar to stay together.

The town of Pisac is over 11,000 feet above sea level and I had been suffering from altitude sickness. My head hurt and I felt exhausted and I could not walk straight. My stomach was God-awful, too.

Miss Reba had appeared at my hut to feed me coca leaves and coca tea. She said a friend in the town told her that an American student was sick.

"Isn't that cocaine?" I asked.

"It's the leaf before it becomes cocaine." Miss

Reba lifted my head from the wool pillow and brings the metal straw and warm cup to me. "Go on," she says. "Drink, be a Peruvian. It's like coffee but better."

I cannot guess Miss Reba's age. She could be much older or much younger and the woman is beautiful in her way. She has that boxy Peruvian face, the wind-worn skin, the dark eyes. Her hair is white and braided and ends below her waist. When she smiles, her front tooth shows an outline of silver.

Miss Reba said her mother was a *curandera* and taught her how to use herbs. My new friend also likes to dry the *Banisteriopsis* vines and smoke them.

"What if I get worse?" I am worried about the coca tea.

She thinks this is very funny. "Then I lose trust," she says. "People will stop asking me to help them and I will become very poor."

MY HUT WAS made of gray stone and dried rectangles of mud. It had one room with tiny windows and a wood door painted turquoise. Sunshine would go through the windows and the open door and cut the shadows. A fireplace in the far-right corner of the room burned dried dung to get the chill off the night and the first of the morning. A damp grass and dirt smell came from the walls and the floor.

I remember my hands shaking. I'd been thinking about my ex-fiancée, my recent and one and only serious breakup. This was a minute or two before Reba had knocked on my door and introduced herself. I couldn't stop the shaking and I folded my fingers into a fist and tucked the fists beneath my arms and out of sight. I do not get very close to people, especially people I don't know. My ex-fiancée used to say I was too withdrawn and too ambivalent. "You want to be close but you always go back and forth." I drove the guy away, I know. But who's perfect?

He used to call me the invisible girl.

Michael Sheetz, that's his name. Michael Sheetz. I mostly refer to him as my ex or my ex-fiancée. I have trouble invoking his actual name. For the first couple of years after our split-up, he was a memory without a face. It's what I do when things get overwhelming, people disappear, at least in my mind.

"Tell me your name," Miss Reba said.

"Liora."

She had finished feeding me the coca tea and the coca leaves and we were now sitting on the mat I use as a bed.

I liked the leaves more than the tea. The leaves go between your cheek and jaw and the juice is the cure. My stomach had relaxed and the headache and dizzy feeling were almost gone.

"Liora is a lovely name," Miss Reba said. She was wearing *ajotas* on her feet, what most locals wear. These are sandals made from recycled tires. Along with the *ajotas* she had on a hand-woven cotton skirt called a *pollera*. "You are lucky to have such a name."

I told her the name was my father's mother's name and my father's mother did not like me having it. My father once said his mother thought the name was her property.

"Are you cold?"

"I'm fine."

"But you shake. How is that fine?"

"I could be a little cold."

"No, you are scared," she said. Her thumb and forefinger guide my chin left and right. She is trying to discover things. The years spent smoking the *caapi* vine itself had worn lines into her face. "I know very well how people get when they are scared. You are twenty...what?"

"...five."

What anthropologists do in the field is observe. We are forever witnesses. We pick a group of people to study and we find patterns to their behaviors and we write many notes about the patterns. It's what cultural anthropologists have done from the start and this is what I did in Pisac. There are rules to field work. The main one says we do not interact with or disturb what we are witnessing.

"I usually can tell about a person," Miss Reba says. She has lighted her pipe. Its thin wood stem is hooked at the corner of her mouth. The smoke has the scent of burning fall leaves. "But I cannot tell about you."

"Maybe I'm not interesting," I say.

"Well now I know you can lie."

Two

WHEN IT RAINS IN TANGIER, it comes with wind and resolve and no sensible person would get in its way. This is what my new friend Dalal has said to me. It's the sort of weather that can go on and on for weeks. Occasionally the rain will flood the streets and bring mud slides. Dalal is visiting her mother who's being treated for pancreatic cancer at the Mohamed V Hospital. Me, I am here for a far more nebulous reason. I am here to go back in time and find the life I gave away. We are both good daughters, Dalal and I, and we are both staying in the Villa de France, a couple of forty-something women who believe our best days may have slipped by us.

Dalal's room is to my left and two doors down. A brown hijab frames her round face. She has the tiniest hands I have ever seen. Dalal also says Matisse stayed at the *Villa de France*, so did Delacroix and many other artists and writers. The first time Matisse visited Tangier, he and his wife Amélie spent much of their vacation in room 36, waiting for the rain to end. Matisse drew the *Paysage vu d'une fenetre* from the window in that room. Last night I watched the lightning whip thready white over St. Andrews Church. But by morning all was quiet.

The streets have now drained off and the day brings sulfur colored clouds in a blue and sun-bright sky. Rain has left the North Atlantic muddy near the shore. Waves are big and ceaseless.

Tangier is on the northwest shoulder of Africa with the Mediterranean to the north and the Atlantic to the west. Most people here call the Mediterranean the straits. At one time or other Tangier has belonged to everybody, the Romans, the Phoenicians, the Portuguese, the Arabs, the English, the French, the Spanish, on and on. People knew, whoever had Tangier had the Mediterranean. And knowing who sailed the Mediterranean and why was a very big deal.

EARLIER THIS MORNING I ran on the Atlantic beach and the sand was wet and firm from last night's rain. The vendors had already set up their carts and umbrellas along the walkway above the beach and there was the smell of meat and fish cooking. I heard my breath and felt the ache leave my thighs and calves, that mortal part of me dropping away.

Most of my time is spent teaching anthropology to undergraduates. I love my students and I love teaching but my job is more brain than body and if I do not run my three a day I start having fantasies about armies of fatty molecules taking over my thighs and stomach. I tell all my students to run, particularly the depressives. I also like hearing skinny nineteen-year-old's say, "How do you stay so thin, Dr. Nowak?"

"Run, run, run, dear."

This beach is nothing like the beaches I am used to in Virginia or the Outer Banks. Tall pine trees are here, pines bent from the ocean wind. What beach has pines? Sea Oats, yes. Sea oats hold the dunes together. But pines are a different matter. Pines should stay in the forest.

While I was running this morning, I saw a young couple coming toward me on horseback. His horse was black and sleek and her horse was gray with a white mane. The man wore a tan fedora, no shirt, and khaki shorts. The woman had on a blue half-buttoned long sleeved shirt that fluttered behind her. Her hair was blond and long and tangled. Her hair lifted here and there in the wind. She, too, wore khaki shorts but she had no shoes.

I had seen this same couple when I checked into the hotel yesterday. They were having an argument. Or that's how it seemed. My field work has taught me not to judge such things too quickly. Behaviors have many meanings and they are bound to many things. But I watched as the woman with the blond hair stiffened her back. She was slim with very delicate features. Her transparent skin showed blue veins on her arms and neck. The man also had pale skin and blond hair and the back of his hair was in a braid and ended an inch below his shoulder blades. Nice looking, I'd thought, both of them, even glamorous. The woman met his anger with a go-on-and-try-it attitude, try it once.

This is the daughter my mother always wanted. She is the daughter who does not take shit. She especially will not take shit from bullies. My father would probably like her too and call her a pistol. The woman has backbone and hair that does what she wants it to do. I always think my parents would have liked me better as a more daring person.

I do not trust my memories of that year at Theresienstadt but I want to say I recall a lot of taunting by my mother and my father. I was never brave enough for them, never clever enough, never beguiling enough.

"You do not see yourself the way others see you," my father would say, a sort of strange pep talk. "You are a beauty – *and* intelligent. And believe me, I'm not someone who flatters for just the sake of it. Your mother and I, we are depending on you. Do you know how hard it is for parents to put their faith and their lives in the hands of a child? It goes against our every instinct. But what can we do? You're what we have."

How does a child say no to that desperation?

Miss Reba is still on my mind, too. I've thought more about her since coming to Tangier than I have in the entire sixteen years since I last saw her. That wonderful face, our talks, her kind manner, from my first step off the plane and onto Tangier she has been with me.

"You never talk about personal things," Miss Reba once said. She'd been sitting next to me on the dirt floor of my hut. Her arms were crossed and pressed to her chest, the pipe at the corner of her mouth. Thick fingers steadied the bowl and the caapi smoke drifted about us. "You do not talk about your mother and father," she said. "Or yourself, your life. Why is this true? Why are you a needless mystery?"

I was beginning to feel calm and the smoke brought images of an October night and of my father Jakub and me burning leaves in our backyard in Norfolk. I told Miss Reba how my parents admired people who were courageous and one step ahead of the herd. My mother and father believed everyone in our family had to be strong every day, every second. Our days in Theresienstadt had demanded it but what I showed them on the outside never matched how I felt on the inside. I was always scared, always unsure.

"Speak about this," Reba said.

"There is nothing to tell."

"Speak about it, anyway."

"We came from Prague," I said.

I used to see buses with painted windows driving through the streets. This was 1944 and many people watched the buses. The windows were painted green so the people inside could not see the city and the people in the city could not see the people inside the buses.

The ones who were taken from us were called *Krankengut*. "Sick goods." There were other names. "Material." "Unnecessary eaters." "Lives unworthy of life."

That same year mother and father and I were brought to Theresienstadt. I had turned thirteen two months before the Nazis had come to our home and pulled us from our beds. Before that, I was like the young blond haired woman I saw this morning on the beach, with that go-on-and-try-it attitude. I had even kicked one of the soldiers in the crotch when he grabbed me from my bed. He was a boy and he laughed and slapped my face and told me that I better be careful.

They took us to Theresienstadt in the bus with the painted windows. This was a transit camp for Czech Jews who were later deported to the killing centers in German occupied Poland, Belorussia, and the Baltic States. Our family spent the last year of the war at Theresienstadt. We remained alive thanks to my father who was a good physician and had been allowed to treat the prisoners. My father was tall and slender with thinning hair and severe blue eyes. A handsome man, I thought, even dashing. But what daughter does not see her father as dashing? Though he was allowed to care for his patients, the Nazis never gave him the medications he needed to keep them alive and well.

"But you survived," Miss Reba said. She was resting against the dried mud wall of my hut. Sunlight went through the windows and the half-opened door and pushed the shadows to the corners.

Reba's short legs were crossed at her ankles and the smoke from her pipe was bright and dusty. "I know many died," she said. "For you and your family to have survived, that is something."

"You would think," I said.

But I said it too softly to hear.

The Nazis brought in the Red Cross and the journalists to watch my father cure the sick. The French press, the Italians, the Americas press, there were no favorites. On those days, medications arrived. The sick got up from their beds and the floors. They walked and smiled for our guests. On those days, my mother and I wore the dresses and shoes that belonged to the people who had taken the trains and left their clothes behind.

Colonel K.P. Kohler oversaw the project, the K.P. for Kurt Paul. He was a slender man like my father but much taller. Over six-three or four, I'm sure. He wore rimless glasses and smoked small black cigars. I remember him as a man who smiled no matter what he was feeling. Smiling was the only facial expression he knew or had been taught. That's what I had thought.

It was Colonel Kohler who decided we would be the Nazis' poster family, the stars of Theresienstadt. That became our job. He moved us into a little wood house in the center of the camp. They painted the wood white and added shutters and real glass to the windows. There were at least four or five other small houses under construction. Something for the Red Cross to see, something for the French and Italian press. It gave the appearance of a new town being built, a bold new departure for prisoners. But the other houses were never finished.

We were the grateful and well-behaved Jews. The Colonel said he pictured us as the Jewish family who could have lived around the corner from anyone, if we had been allowed to do that.

"I can't believe what we have here," my mother said. She and my father and I were looking about the small house and marveling at its luxury and our good luck. On reflection, it wasn't much. But compared to our apartment in Prague and the barracks in Theresienstadt, it was a castle, a luxury beyond luxuries. Our apartment in Prague had been nothing more than a single room with my mother and father sleeping in one corner and me sleeping in the corner diagonally opposite from them. But our house in the camp had a bedroom for each of us and a kitchen and a living area. I recall Mother turning to me and I heard the anxiousness in her voice. "He likes you, Liora. This gentleman, this Colonel, he likes you, I know it. You must help us. Are you listening? You must help our family survive."

I think I remember the Colonel Kohler saying

that to me, what mother believed. "Such a pretty, well-behaved girl," he'd said. "A special girl must have a special house." Or maybe I made it up, I don't know. I have shut those times away. Some days, though, I was the family hero. Other days, my father thought we were being traitors to the other prisoners. "Traitors to our people," he had called it.

The people in Prague saw our photographs in the newspaper and sent us hate mail. There was envy in the camp, too; some called mother a Nazi whore. They said father was Hitler's physician. Most people declared me the victim, the innocent child swayed by her parents to do the bidding of Colonel Kohler. We were despised, vilified, we were traitors and Nazi lovers.

I understand the anger, the envy.

But I agree with my father, I would do it again.

I am sure my reason for being in Tangier will ultimately keep my past in the past where it belongs. *Yesterday looks different in the present.* Now the doors are opened, the cage unlocked. I am glad I discussed my time in Theresienstadt with Miss Reba. I do not want to be alone in this. Even in my memories, she is a protector.

I AM SITTING on a white wood beach chair overlooking the North Atlantic. Waves are breaking into foam and spreading over already wet sand. I am waiting for Dalal to show me the Café Hafa on the Rue Mohammed Tazi. The café has been in Tangier since the twenties and they are supposed to brew the best mint tea in town. It is midmorning and the sun is strong and the wind from the ocean whips up bits of the sand and flaps the edges of the umbrellas that shade the food carts. My hair is covered with a peach colored scarf, my version of the hijab. The ends of the scarf flutter about my shoulders. I don't want the people of Tangier to think I am thumbing my nose at their culture. I also have a pair of those big sunglasses Jacqueline Kennedy likes to wear. Or Onassis. But I will always think of her as a Kennedy. With the scarf and the glasses, only my nose, lips and chin are visible.

At the hotel, last night Dalal told me, "Ramadan begins September 17th, the day after tomorrow. You should not go out at night." Dalal was shuffling a deck of Tarot cards. My friend believes she can tell fortunes and she was arranging the cards on a round wood table. "People get robbed or beaten," Dalal said. "Or worse. We are not ourselves when our meals get disrupted. It's a difficult time for everyone. Best to stay in the hotel."

"What gets them angry?" Now I was curious.

"Many things."

"No, really. What?"

"Western women. Also, Jews and Americans."

THREE

DALAL IS LOOKING AT ME with those big questioning eyes. "You're *not* married?"

"I'm not against marriage," I say to her.

"You must want babies, yes?"

"I've thought about babies." And this is partly true. My ex-fiancée Michael and I used to talk of marriage and children in our college days. The infamous Michael Sheetz, the now-I-love-you-now-I-don't Michael Sheetz. I do think about adopting a child. There are many orphaned children in Peru. But I can't get babies past the thinking stage and that's been close to twenty years.

"You can't have children?"

"No, I can have them."

"I need to tell your fortune." There is frustration in Dalal's voice. "We have only known each other for a few days but I can see our differences. My husband, may God care for his soul, used to tell me I wear my life on my sleeve. But you do not show yourself too easily. Am I right? Perhaps the cards will help me know you."

"I am not so different from many women in America," I say. "But in some ways, I am very different. I've been engaged and almost married. I have had other gentleman friends but I did not give them the time they needed. Or that's what I've been told. My work gets in the way of relationships. It's difficult to explain the importance of my work to others. I probably cannot give men the time they require. 'Beware of people who have a calling.' Do you know a calling?"

"A passion? Like religious people?"

"Yes, it's that."

We are on the terrace of the Café Hafa. Our waiter, Kamal, says the café opened in 1921 and nothing has changed but the people. He is very young and has black short cropped hair and a beard. He also has lovely dark eyes. The terrace is on the side of a hill and customers sip mint tea and look at the strait of Gibraltar and at each other. Eucalyptus and umbrella pines shade us. White seagulls glide over the water and through the sunlight. Kamal says the writers Paul Bowles and William Burroughs like the Hafa. Jack Kerouac liked it, too.

Right now, I'm sitting here with Dalal and waiting for my tea to cool and watching the honey bees balance on the rim of the glass to get the sugar. Dalal has on her brown hijab and sunglasses. Mint tea is the big thing here. Kamal tells us they have made their tea the same way since 1921. The other big thing here is kif. It's a powder made from the flower of the female marijuana plant. But I am not very good at picking out who is smoking what.

"Does your job give you good money?" Dalal says.

"It gives me enough money. I have a small house not too far away from the college, about three miles. I run there in the morning."

"Even when it's cold?"

"Whatever it is, I run."

"That's very commendable. I should exercise more."

"I should tell you, my house is not glamorous. It's filled with old furniture and a small piano I have never played. But I imagine myself playing it. And I am always very good when I imagine it. I also have many pictures of childhood friends in Prague. Oh, and I like opera, particularly *Madam Butterfly*. I love *Madam Butterfly*."

"Maria Callas?"

"Tamaki Miura. But the other one is very good."

"Would you like me to tell your fortune?" Dalal loves her Tarot cards. And she refuses to give up on this fortune telling business.

"I'm not that sort of person," I say.

"People like fortune telling."

"I know they do."

"But you don't, Dr. Nowak?"

"Call me, Liora. Fifty-fifty."

"But what's the harm, Liora?"

Dalal is right, of course. I am notorious at keeping people at arm's length. And for what purpose? I do not need to insult this sweet lady who so obviously wants to be my friend.

"No harm," I tell her and force a smile.

AN ANTHROPOLOGIST IS more comfortable in the corner of the room. This is the nature of people who become anthropologists. I was a good witness as a girl of thirteen in Theresienstadt. Mother, Father and I had to be vigilant to stay alive. We fussed over the nuances of unremarkable sentences, the significance of a half-smile, the glance held a beat too long, the occasional gift, the reprimand, the unnecessary compliment. We did not want to find ourselves being herded onto a train and toted off to the killing camps. We had seen the people in the cattle cars. Their arms and fingers and legs between the gray wood slats, their eyes frantic and searching for help, for another day, another chance. I remember the smell of them, the urine, the sweat. I heard the shouts and cries.

We learned to take meaning out of what had no meaning. We studied the ones next to us and the ones who had power over us and the ones who thought we had power over them. Everyone in the camp thought everyone else was getting the better deal, and everyone knew we were getting the *best* deal. To live in one of those little white houses being built in the center of the camp was both a wish come true and a betrayal. Our good luck depended on the day and my parents' feelings. More than a few prisoners despised us. My mother I and were seen as whores – not by everyone, but enough of them thought that. You could cut their envy with an axe. It was our world then, the power and the helplessness. No other measure could be found in Theresienstadt. People tried to have a bearable life in a bad situation.

This is why Colonel Kohler troubled my parents so much. There was nothing about him to judge, not a hint, nothing from which we could extract meaning. His facial expression never changed nor did the tone of his voice. He was what my father called,

"Chipper," always a smile, always a soft pleasant greeting.

I was also troubled by the Colonel, but in a different way. He would watch me. He could be talking on the phone or talking to my parents or to one of the guards, it did not matter. If I was nearby, he would watch. At first, I did not know what to do about it or how to feel. I'd looked at the ground or out a window. Then I learned to stare back at him. But he was not like me. The Colonel wouldn't look away.

I am forty-two years old now. And I'm a better witness at forty-two than at thirteen. This is why I am good at anthropology. And how bizarre, really. It was the anthropologists from the *Kaiser-Wilhelm-Institut für Anthropologie* who had assisted the Third Reich in mapping out the racial characteristics of the German nation. It was the anthropologists who instructed the SS doctors on how to pursue the ethnographic inquiry. Anthropology was one of the main disciplines that had advocated the sterilization of criminals, the mentally ill, the genetically deformed, and so on. This history has not escaped me. What can I do but attempt to right a wrong?

An anthropologist must always be vigilant and if you are vigilant by nature you cannot be vigilant here and not there. I've learned how to become the person you do not notice but the person who notices you.

❖ ❖ ❖

"I AM VERY good at fortunes," Dalal says. "In our village, women want the cards to reveal secrets about their husbands. Men want this for their wives. Very common. Over the years, the cards have reveal many interesting situations."

"Correct predictions?"

"Oh yes, many correct predictions. You cannot imagine how many husbands and wives have affairs with their spouse's brother or sister."

"I don't think you need fortune telling for that."

I can smell the sweetness of my mint tea and would like to have a sip of it but I do not know what to do about the bees on the rim of my glass. I believe that shooing bees away from your glass is asking for trouble. Maybe this is the reason for the kif.

"I have been told I am too personal," Dalal says. Her dark brown hijab is an oval frame about her face.

"You are very hard on yourself." I say.

"It's an unpleasant habit." Dalal gives me a nervous wave of her hand as if to dismiss the whole idea of fortune telling. "My husband, may he rest in peace, he always said I was too personal for my own good. 'Dalal,' he'd say, 'You must stop with your absurd questions. You bother the neighbors.

Women who bother the neighbors are not looked upon in a good light.' My husband was a wise man."

"I didn't realize your husband had passed on."

"His heart. He had rheumatic fever as a child."

"I'm sorry. How old was he?"

"Forty-five. But I am at peace with it. He was not that good a husband."

"Do you have children?"

"A boy. But he is like his father." Dalal removes a bee from the rim of her tea glass with a thumb and forefinger and flicks it away. The move is casual but swift and impressive. She sips her tea and says, "Men think women are what do you call it? Inessential? Is that the right word?"

"You know your English," I tell her. Then I say, "Your boy, he's not with you?"

"My Aabid has school. He's staying with his father's sister while I look after my mother. I miss him greatly."

"I bet you're a wonderful mother."

"With God's help."

The water in the straits goes from turquoise to navy to a muddy color. Back and forth, back and forth. It must depend on the sun and the shadow, I'm thinking. The play between shade and light can show things not revealed in any other way. I see why people look at the water. I am hypnotized by it, by its beauty and by its changes. The straits are a mystery that is always revealing the next layer and the next. We know there are transformations to come, that the shade and the light will not keep to the same patterns. I am captured by the shifting of it all.

Dalal is studying my face.

"...what?"

"Come see me tomorrow night. I will use the cards and read your fortune," Dalal says. "Most people think fortune telling is an amusement." She nods her head left to right at the idea as if to imply, maybe so-maybe not. "Rich people invite me to their parties to entertain the guests," she says. "They pay very well. Not you, though. You don't pay. For you it's free. It's an amusement, you see. I am an amusement, that's all. Inessential. It's a way to pass the time, the fortune telling. I say this because I do not want to cause you discomfort."

"I am very fine with it," I say. I give her a smile that is so phony-baloney a person could peel it off and put it on a sandwich.

"You are sure, Liora?"

"I'm never sure. But I am willing."

I wonder what Dalal truly thinks of fortune telling? It is still difficult for me to believe she can do what she said she does or has the powers she said she has. Maybe they are not powers; I am not sure what to call them.

But I know what I believe. It is the unassuming person who surprises me the most. Take Miss Reba, for instance. I do not think I would notice her on the street. She has a quiet manner about her and she is the sort of person who'd pass by and no one would know it.

Dalal is looking at me.

"This will be fun," she says and wants me to agree.

"I can't wait."

"Oh good."

IF PEOPLE LOOK my way a moment longer than I think they should, I become uncomfortable. And since people are always looking at other people, I am forever uncomfortable. I am far too private a person. I know it and I know why and I am always trying to overcome it. I push myself to reveal myself. Perhaps my time in Theresienstadt helped to seal me up. Our family would not be the first survivors to keep our distance from others. I have read about such cases in the journals, the survivor families who treat one another as strangers. Parents and children who go days without talking. I guard my entrance to becoming known. And my looks have conspired with me. I am neither attractive nor hideous and because I have no qualities that entice the passers-by, the beau, the possible friend, I am invisible to them. Uninteresting. That's it exactly, the blessing and the curse of it, I am a visually uninteresting person. I can lose myself in a crowd of two.

But I am not above being a paradox. Yes, even someone like me. No one can be expected to relinquish their last threads of narcissism. I have never given up the hope and the horror that I will be looked at by someone. Oh, not admired, mind you. That would be too much to ask. And I certainly will not be seen as beloved, but I am an honest person and as an honest person I confess that I do harbor the secret hope of being looked at longer than necessary.

DALAL TAPS MY hand with the tip of her forefinger and glances at the white archway behind me. The young man and woman who are staying on our floor in the Villa de France have just walked onto the terrace. She is wearing sunglasses and a white linen dress and red leather sandals. The sandals show her toes and the vague blue veins along the tops and sides of her feet. Wind from the straits flicks strands of her blond hair across her face. The woman walks with her head tilted and slightly down. I get the feeling she does not like being seen, either. She is a step or two behind the young man who has on a gray shirt with the sleeves rolled to the elbows. He also wears the same fedora I saw this morning at the beach. His blond braid ends at the middle of his back. They sit at the table in front of us and face the straits. Palms and low flowering hedges surround them. The man and the woman are what I think of when I think of a romantic couple. They are models in a magazine, that's how I picture them. But the woman seems more withdrawn than she did this morning.

Perhaps I live too much in my own fantasies.

"His name is Willem and her name is Eloise. Very exquisite, aren't they?"

Dalal has leaned toward me to whisper this. She says, "They have the room next to mine."

"So you've said." I want to hear more about Willem and Eloise but I hate appearing too eager.

"They are very noisy."

"They fight?"

"Sometimes. But mostly they pick at each other."

"What do you mean pick?" I say.

"Fuss. Nothing is ever right between them."

"That's worse than being alone."

"My marriage was no different," Dalal says.

"They must have their moments."

"That's noisy, too."

"Oh, you are so bad."

Dalal puts her fingers to her mouth to stop a laugh. "Young people never sleep," she says and rolls her eyes. "As awful as my marriage was, my husband would still wake me twice a night. He liked to poke at me." Dalal is talking and thinking about this. She has a tiny smile at the right corner of her mouth. "I'd say, 'Go back to sleep, Ahmed. You must work tomorrow and you will be tired.' And he'd say, 'What do you think I am trying to do? Now be quiet, Dalal. Help your husband.' What was I supposed to tell him? He provided for his family. Men know one day they will not be able to do it. So, they do it as much as they can before they cannot do it anymore."

"I don't know whether I could be so considerate."

"Ahmed would also look after me and our son. He was not completely without his good points. Many times, he would bring me presents or take Aabid and me to the park or bring us a pastry he knew we enjoyed. This was a mostly good man, except when he drank. When he drank, my son and I had to stay away until he fell asleep."

I still have my silk peach scarf about my head and my shoulders and I am also wearing my sunglasses. Clouds move under the sun and put shadows on the water and the white concrete of the terrace. The edges of my scarf twist in the wind and I keep smoothing the scarf with the flat of my hand.

"He hurt her last night," Dalal says.

"Who? You mean Willem?"

"They argued for a long time. Then I heard a big thump on the wall. Then they were quiet. Nobody talked. I think he hurt her."

Four

THESE CURVED AND NARROW STREETS are not the best for a woman by herself. That's what Dalal tells me but her warning has more to do with wandering about at night than during the day. This is the oldest part of Tangier and the old part is called the Medina. Maybe I shouldn't be here. I am sure it is dangerous but it's also very ancient and romantic.

Afternoon sunshine has come to the streets in angles, light that breaks the shadow, light brilliant on the smooth white sides of buildings and the gray and the tan awnings of shops that line both sides of Le Petite Socco.

Today I am thinking about my breakup with Michael, what we said to each other and what I had done to end the pain of it.

"But I did love you," he had said.

"Did? What do you mean did?"

"You're not an easy person."

"And what are you? Gandhi?"

My breakup with Michael Sheetz. He smelled of Brylcreem and he'd chewed Dentyne to hide the cigarettes. When I knew him in the early fifties he was mostly teeth and long bones. We were both seniors at Virginia Commonwealth University and both had majors in anthro. Michael was always buying movie magazines and he dressed like Rock Hudson or Gordan MacRae. He had a closet of gray flannel slacks and checkered sports jackets. His favorite songs were Dean Martin's "That's Amore" and Perry Como's "Don't Let the Stars Get in Your Eyes."

We would make love in my dorm on Friday afternoons. Afterward he would smoke a Lucky Strike cigarette and sing "That's Amore." Michael loved that song. He would sing it to me very seriously, the way people do in the movies. He was the first and only boy who ever said he loved me and I believed him right away and I thought love meant he would love me regardless of anything.

"Maybe marriage has you nervous," I'd said. I was twenty-one and already an expert witness to the unpleasantness of my life.

"Why don't you look at yourself?"

"Who's calling off the marriage?" I said.

"You don't talk. It's like you hide in a corner or something."

"Oh? What are we doing now?"

"You know what I mean." Michael inhaled his cigarette and gave me his best exasperated look. He sat cross-legged and naked in the bed, the white sheet to his waist, an amber colored ashtray balanced on the hidden mount that was his knee. His dark hair lay Brylcreem shiny to his forehead. "I noticed how we don't have normal talks," my so-called fiancé said, exhaling thready lines of smoke through his nose.

"I'm serious, okay? If you say anything, it's because I've spent an hour forcing it out of you."

"I didn't realize I was such a burden."

"This isn't easy for me, Liora."

"Well you're doing good."

"You live on another planet."

"This is about marrying me," I said.

"Isn't marriage forever? People think about things."

"I knew it."

"You're like a shadow. The invisible girl."

I'D BEEN VERY young then but I knew I wasn't Miss Congeniality. Now I am forty-two and I know that nothing has really changed. One can go after this job and that, one can be assertive and charming – and *never* get personal. Oh yes. Do not mistake a good set of social skills for revealing oneself. I know many socially skilled women who, when I think about, I do not know at all. I know a woman whose daughter is named Taylor or Butler or one of those southern names, but I had to find out from others that Taylor or Butler was a young lesbian who got discovered in her dorm with another young woman and became so humiliated she overdosed on tranquilizers.

Never confuse invisible with a lack of charm.

Theresienstadt has kept me from people who were not there and couldn't imagine what it was like being there. But Theresienstadt has also kept me from people who were there and wanted to reminisce.

What else is left?

THE AMERICANS RESCUED us toward the end of 1945. My parents have stayed healthy thanks to Daddy. He is a man who believes in vitamins and exercise and I am sure he will keep the two of them alive despite themselves.

We have lived in America for over twenty years. My parents have a brick rancher in the Talbot Park section of Norfolk, Virginia. Mother likes to garden and Father likes to golf. When I left them to go to college, I left them for good. We have Thanksgiving dinners together but I do not visit them outside that holiday and they do not visit me. We remind each other too much of our year in Theresienstadt. If my mother and father could live separately, they would do it. I suspect my parents stay together not out of companionship but because they are getting older.

Though some die alone, nobody likes it.

Mother will write to me every two months or so. Her letters discuss my weight and hair issues and my social problems. "I am worried about your skinny arms, Liora," she will write.

I can picture her placing a manicured thumb and forefinger about my wrist. This is what she does at Thanksgiving. Mother likes to dress in a long silk sleeved blouse with stiff high collars and a strand or two of tiny pearls. Her nails are clipped and curved and polished with clear lacquer.

"Look at your refugee hair." she says. "You must always think about your future. Your father and I won't be alive forever, you know."

"Speak for yourself, Elzbieta," my father will tell her.

Mother ignores him. "How are you going to get a husband with hair like that?" she says to me. "It's too curled and out of sorts."

Sometimes my mother and I will be alone in the kitchen and she'll ask me if I ever hear from Colonel Kohler, a letter, a card.

"Why would I hear from that beast?"

"He always liked you," she'd whisper. "It's what saved us."

Holidays.

BUT WHEN I was a twenty-one-year-old girl and in bed with Michael Sheetz I was mostly thinking about his promise to marry me and my life as a wife and a mother.

"This is very funny, you know?" I said this while lying next to him. The sheet was tucked about my neck to hide my far too white and skinny body. I could not disguise the hurt feelings in my voice. "I don't think I heard the 'shadow' thing when you were climbing on top of me, the 'invisible girl' thing. I heard a lot of moaning, I definitely heard that. And I heard a lot of 'oh baby' and 'oh honey,' but I don't remember hearing anything about how I am like a shadow, an invisible girl."

He ignored what I was saying and lifted my left hand from under the sheet and pointed to the six tattooed numbers on my forearm. The tattoo was given to me in Theresienstadt.

"How did I miss this?" he had asked.

"Some things you share, some things you don't."

Michael and I had made love before but my

arms and my upper body were always clothed. A nightgown, a long-sleeved blouse, a pullover. I had told him I was shy and he had understood or that was what he had said. It was the fifties and most men and women were shy in the fifties and turned off the lights. People liked hiding in the dark. They liked pretending they were anonymous. "You don't know me and I do not know you and we are going to engage in this very intimate act and after it's over we will pretend it did not happen." That was the fifties. But on this particular afternoon I thought, I am going to marry Michael Sheetz and I should learn to trust him. I should let him see me Oliver Cromwell style, warts and all. I was prepared not to cringe at his condolences, but that didn't happen.

"I want to say the right thing," he said.

"You don't have to say anything. It's done."

Michael inhaled his cigarette. His lips went thin. "How can you not share that with me, not give me a clue?"

We had never talked about the camp or my religion. I don't think either of us was all that reli-gious. But I don't know, really. I was so happy a boy loved me and wanted to marry me. I did not bother with what my parents would have considered the important questions.

"What are you?" I said, "A Baptist, an Episcopalian? What, exactly?"

"Well my parents are Methodists."

"So, you are what?"

"What they are, I guess."

"Okay. I am from another planet."

"See," Michael said. He waved a forefinger at me as though I had helped prove a point. It came out of nowhere. He snubbed his cigarette into the amber colored ashtray still propped on the bed sheet that covered the mount of his knee. "This is what I'm talking about," he said and let the last of the smoke leave his mouth and nose. "You've got an attitude. You're either totally silent or you think everybody is so totally amusing. We're all too cute for words."

"Why are we arguing over this?" I had raised my left forearm and was pointing to the tattoo. Now I had a mission.

"Because you don't trust me," Michael said. "Because more often than not I feel on the outside with you. I hate saying that, hate admitting it to myself. Why get married if we're going to stay strangers?"

I did not look at him. Tears were hot on the rims of my eyes. And I hated these feelings I could not control. I hated anyone to see my feelings, especially clueless Michael Sheetz. It embarrassed me. It showed I cared about him. And, of course, I did care. People do not turn off loving somebody so quickly.

"…Liora." He reached out for my hand again.

"Maybe you're right," I said, pouty myself by then. "We can't have you marrying an invisible girl. What sort of life would that be?"

This was the talk we had a week before our wedding. Not a month before our wedding, not the second date. This was the day before my parents and his parents were coming to Richmond and staying at the Jefferson on my almost overdrawn savings account. Michael Sheetz and I were supposed to get married at the old City Hall on East Broad Street.

The more I think about my relationship with Michael the more I see him as "the invisible *boy*." I think invisible boys and invisible girls are drawn to one another. I did not know that then but I know that now. I know there are choices going on. Maybe we are not consciously aware of the choices but these things do go on inside us. It's true. Any good anthropologists will tell you this one simple rule: *birds of a feather really do flock together*. Invisible boys and invisible girls know they will not be discovered if they find their own kind.

This last time Michael and I were in bed together was the most talking Michael ever did with me. It was a month's worth of talking in twenty minutes. Michael and I always loved to do things that did not need us to talk to one another, the movies, reading books together, doing crossword puzzles. I cannot even remember him saying, "What's a four-letter word for such and such."

We didn't even say anything to each other when we made love. Wait, that's not true. Michael would sometimes say, "Did you finish?" That was the big question. *Did you finish, hon?*

I think Michael wanted to get himself loose from me, it's what our last talk had been about. We were both scared, or that's how I think about it now. That's what it was, pure and simple. I sometimes think I would have done the same thing to him. The boy just beat me to it.

I think about Michael too much; I have for years, twenty years too much. I imagine him as a balding man with a belly the size of a soccer ball and thin white legs. I imagine he has three hyperactive children and a wife with thick arms and too much eye shadow, and she will not stop talking. I always smile at that. I picture him shutting out his wife's chatter and remembering the invisible girl.

AN HOUR OR two after Michael said he'd changed his mind about marrying me, I had gone to the corner 7-11 and bought a big box of wine. Most girls in the dorm bought wine in boxes instead of bottles because you got more wine in a box and the wine was cheaper than the wine you got in bottles. The wine box also had a beautiful photo of wet green grapes with the word "chardonnay" written in gold script. The outside of the box appealed to our esthetics and the inside did what we wanted it to do.

By ten that evening I had finished the wine or very close to it and I locked myself in the bathroom at the end of the hall and began cutting on both arms. My feelings were not clear about this and I was not very good at it. I cut horizontally across my wrists, not vertically. And I should have cut deeper. Today I know better and I would get in a tub and use warm water to keep the blood from clotting. The staff at the Medical College of Virginia called what I had done a "cry for help." I thought of that as somewhere between being an actress and a coward.

Now I see there is no use in being brave and dead.

"You're a crazy person," my father said.

"I don't need to hear this."

"You need to hear it a lot."

Daddy was sitting at the side of my hospital bed on a bright orange vinyl chair with aluminum legs and armrests. His voice was quiet so the older woman in the bed next to us would not hear him.

But the older woman slept on her back with her mouth open and she could not hear anything except her own noise.

The nurse had just pulled the ceiling curtain around us for privacy.

"You did not try this stunt in Theresienstadt," my father said.

"A stunt? Is that what we're calling it? My stunt."

"You were strong in Theresienstadt."

"Other people were suffering."

"Other people suffer here."

I looked down at the bandages on my wrists. The nurse must have given me a sedative. I felt like I was in a dream and could not open my eyes all the way. Then I said, "Did you tell Mama?" My words sounded slurred.

"You told me not to, so I didn't."

Father treated every situation as a moral lesson. Mother treated everything as a drama. She would have cried at my bedside and fluttered a hand in front of her face to keep her mascara from running. I am sure she could have persuaded the nurse to give her the bed next to mine. My father was more the teacher, the guy who was all logic. "What can we learn from this?" he'd ask. "Don't let this moment go to waste, Liora."

"Am I an invisible girl?" I wanted to know.

"That's the medication talking."

"Michael said I was invisible."

"Michael's an asshole."

I remember watching Daddy's face change. First, he was stern and perhaps frightened for me. Then he was sad. Or his face had turned sad. He brought my hand up to his lips and kissed my fingers. He pressed my hand to his cheek. His skin was warm and I could feel the bristle start of his beard. He stayed quiet and watched me with those severe blue eyes and I thought I had done something wrong.

"You're as visible as I am," he said.

"I think Michael's right."

"It's a memory, Liora."

"It doesn't feel that way."

"Some memories are ghosts." Daddy's aftershave smelled of cinnamon. It mixed with the disinfectant of the E.R. "You know the ghost is there but you cannot see him," Daddy had said. "You know he is real but he cannot be touched. Some memories are like that."

"We should hire an investigator." I said.

"To do what?"

"To find the invisible girl," I said. "I'll pay you back."

"Investigators are very expensive."

"What are we worth?"

❖ ❖ ❖

WIND FROM THE Atlantic and the straits runs the walls of the Medina and the sand whirls about the narrow street along the Le Petite Socco. I feel it at my cheeks, my chin. It pricks and stings like tiny knives. Locals do not seem to notice this wind, this sand, or if they do notice, they do not care.

We've had many investigators over twenty-nine years. We thought the Colonel was in Rio de Janeiro, Morro do San Paulo, on and on. Nepal, for God's sake. I have traveled to at least two other places since these investigations started. Costa Rica for one; Geneva for another. The Colonel knows to keep ahead of things. My father and I hired these investigators to find him and, indirectly, the invisible girl. To get the invisible girl visible again is everything. I cannot tell you how much that image haunts me, the invisible girl. My father wants for me what I want for myself. He wants to help me get my life back.

Our current investigator is Leon Nauman, retired cop and a friend and patient of my father's. Leon says he has found Colonel Kohler. Leon says the Colonel is calling himself Hartmut Becker now. Leon says the man lives here in Tangier. But Leon does not tell me where in Tangier. He just tells me not to worry. Passports and names always change with a man like the Colonel. He is a master of his neighborhood and staying one step ahead of whoever wants him jailed or dead or both. Kohler is also under the protection of the CIA. They keep track of him—who he knows, who he sees. But other countries want him and do not care who protects him.

FIVE

From atlantic beach, I can see Robinson's on the hill to my left. A sandy path goes from the beach to the top of the hill and there are large rocks and brush and pine trees. Robinson's is a restaurant that has been here since the mid-forties when Tangier was called the International Zone. Dalal has told me that, too. The French and the Spanish and the British, and God knows who else, would drive to Robinson's for its chicken tajine with olives and pickled lemons, the Harira soup made from vegetables, meat, rice and spice. Dalal used to take a train from her home outside Casablanca just for the grilled sardines stuffed with chermoula. And always customers would have a side order of kesra and a pastry. The restaurant is a long and low white building with a gray stone fence in front of it.

Today Robinson's is closed.

Ramadan has started. It's the Islamic month of fasting and the fasting is from dawn to sunset. After that, people go to a big town square and eat under a dark sky with lots of candlelight. Dalal tells me it is very lovely. Muslims will pray most of the day and eat most of the night. Many have trouble sleeping. For one month, everybody's world is turned around.

It is a time for sacrifice and the cleansing of the soul. People will ask God to forgive their sins and guide their lives.

Have I been the best person I can be?

How can I be a better person?

The second week into Ramadan cab drivers are falling asleep at the wheel. Vendors stop giving you deals. Restaurants close down during the day. Friends may start getting annoyed at friends and even people they do not know. Tourists are frowned upon. Physical attacks and robberies go up. If a friend happens to see another friend at a café having a cup of tea during daylight hours, tables may be overturned, lectures may occur.

"Why do you drink tea when you should be in prayer?" the non-tea drinking friend will say. "Is this how you show respect?"

It's a serious time for Moroccan Muslims, for

all Muslims. People who live in Tangier and who are not Muslims try to stay out of the way.

We eat in our rooms.

Ramadan reminds me of Catholic Lent and Yom Kippur. But Jews fast and pray for twenty-four hours and that's it. Any longer would get our mothers and grandmothers nagging us about how thin we look. "Here, eat this," they'd say. "God won't mind you having a little nosh." Yom Kippur is our Day of Atonement. And like the Muslims, we pray and confess our sins and ask God for forgiveness and guidance.

My father says everybody wants forgiveness. He says we want to unburden ourselves to God. We want relief from our sins. We want to do better and we want God to guide us and see us doing better.

I am not a religious person.

Daddy does not understand this. Mother does not care to think about it. They believe my atheism comes from some defect in them or their parenting. A rogue gene, perhaps. Not enough suckle time at the breast. Mother and Father argue over who is responsible for the chink in my character.

"We should have gone to shul in a regular way," Father says to Mother.

"The rabbi kept rubbing against me," she says. "Don't you remember? Who can go to a shul when the rabbi wants to have sex with you?"

"There is more than one shul in the world, Elzbieta."

"We should have prayed more at home."

Whatever the defect, whatever the reason, I go through my days without the assistance of worship. My parents should give credit where credit is due. It's my choice and my doing. I do not get it, this religion business. I have friends who are physicians and have pulled misshaped babies from many wombs. There are babies who come into the world with no arms and stumps for feet, babies with hearts that will never work right. A woman friend once delivered twins who were connected at the forehead. I have also dealt with my own horrors. I was in Theresienstadt where a middle-aged officer had sex with children. I had watched a prison guard push an inmate to the ground and put a shovel to his throat and rock back and forth on the handle until the prisoner died.

Where is God? We need to talk.

IT IS TWILIGHT in Tangier now and the sky over the Atlantic is streaked pink and orange and deep, deep blue. I am holding my sandals in my hand and walking barefoot on the beach. The sand is still warm from the day.

Dalal will read my future tonight. Isn't it peculiar how fortune tellers gain their credibility by telling us not about our future but about our past? The fortune teller will start with a vague observation. "You have been feeling sad today," they will say. Or better still, "These recent days have been a concern to you." This is followed by cautious probing but always very generally. "I see a loss or perhaps an argument."

Knowing this scene will happen tonight has started me thinking about the past, especially my days as a thirteen-year-old in the camp. These thoughts are different than my usual thoughts about that horrid place, that endless year. My usual thoughts about that place have minimal feelings. It is as if I am looking at other people's photographs, other people's babies. Do not get me wrong. I am forever caught in Theresienstadt, forever obsessing. But I keep that time in my head and away from my heart. These recent thoughts, though, have feelings woven into them.

The Nazis had a logic of their own. Amid the genocide, they wanted the world to see their practical and humanitarian nature. A productive, healthier, and more efficient society, this is what they wanted. More actually. They wanted my family to see the logic in it and to agree with them. Years later I am still stunned by what the Nazis saw as their rightness of purpose. They wanted the world to say, "Oh yes, you are doing what we do not have the will to do. We, too, want criminals gone from our gene pool, the mentally deficient, the sick, the handicapped, sterilize them all." But sterilization was not as sure as murder. Then the list expanded to the homosexuals, the aged, the Jews, the Catholics, the Gypsies, the Slavs, the Italians, the French, the Ukrainians, the Poles, the Serbs, a very long and dedicated list.

I cannot begin to understand this. And I am not a stupid person. I received my Ph.D. from Southern Illinois. I am a cultural anthropologist but I still do not understand that dark absurdist behavior. Maybe I should say, I know nothing about the Nazis that satisfies me. There is no answer that allows me to say, "Yes, that is it. I can stop now. I can turn over and tuck my blanket about my shoulders and sleep well tonight. I will put that life aside and say this is what their behavior was and this is how it began. Now we can stop it from ever happening again."

But those of us who lived through Theresienstadt and the other camps were not survivors. Where did people get that name? Survivor. I do not think any of us survived. There were simply dead bodies and breathing bodies.

Do I want to stir up all of that again?

Off and on I have wondered why I am letting

Dalal tell my fortune. Maybe I know why, or have a guess. I am a long way from my home and I like having a good friend. Why not let her enjoy herself?

THE YOUNG BLOND woman is sitting on the beach. Eloise. Her hands are locked about her raised knees. She is also barefoot. And like me, she's wearing her sunglasses even though the sun is almost gone. Wind from the Atlantic shakes the hem of her full white skirt.

Eloise is watching me. Or at least her face is pointed in my direction. It's hard to know what her eyes are doing behind her sunglasses. I do not wave to people. Rather, I do not initiate waving. I've no idea why. It does seem rude and I am not a rude person. Eloise lifts her hand tentatively toward me and I smile at her. She looks very alone sitting there on the empty beach. I glance about for Willem but I don't see him.

"It's so beautiful here," Eloise says.

I smile again and start to pass her.

"...this time of day," she says. "...the way the sky is..." These sentences have no beginnings and vanish before they end. Eloise cups her hand over her sunglasses to look at me. "I'm not from Tangier, either."

"Am I so obvious?" I say.

"I'm from Jersey. Camden."

"I'd thought European."

"My husband is European," Eloise says and brushes strands of hair away from her face, strands tangled by the wind. She is thin and pale and much prettier up close. "I met Willem in Berlin the summer before last, mother and I. My mother thought Willem was very handsome."

"What did you think?"

"He is handsome, isn't he?"

"You're a lovely looking couple," I tell her.

"That's what mother says."

A portable radio is propped upright in the sand next to Eloise. The DJ has an English accent. A light but constant static plays about his talk. He's saying, "...new one from Wings, 'Band on the Run.' On R...N...I." This is followed by the slow drifting sound of a guitar.

I tell Eloise I did not know Tangier had an English-speaking radio station, one that played popular music.

"It's not from here," she says. "It's North Sea International." Eloise points toward the Atlantic. She has on an oversized blue cotton shirt and the sleeves are folded neatly to the elbow. There is a speckled bruise on her right wrist, three or four oblong shapes. The shapes are a purple greenish color. "They're on a ship and they park out there," Eloise says. "You can barely see it. Sometimes they stay for a month, sometimes more. I come to the beach in the evening because I can hear the music better. They do news, too. Last month all they talked about was Watergate and Nixon."

I have always been a witness. I become the witness again, the one who notices this young woman. How she glided onto the bright terrace at the Café Hafa yesterday, her head tilted slightly, the wife who followed her husband but did not want to be seen. In and out of the sunlight, passing under the shaded palms, the two of them were a private caravan. Now we meet on the beach and I see her bruised wrist, the three or four oblong shapes that fit about the bone like a bracelet of shadows. Maybe she is not as brave as I had originally thought.

I sit down beside Eloise. I do not look at her but I sit like her. My arms are about my raised knees. Bony pale feet peek out beneath my dark skirt. I join her by sitting the way she sits and by looking at what she is looking at. We watch the Atlantic together, the white and constant waves.

I am waiting for the right moment to look at her.

"Are you homesick?" I want to know.

"I miss my baby brother."

"What's his name?"

"Max…Maxwell. He's twelve."

"Tell me about Max."

"He sends me drawings," Eloise says. She is still looking at the ocean but she smiles at the thought of Max. "They're picture letters," Eloise says. "He likes drawing what he did that day or what he saw. He sent me a picture of traffic last week. You know, cars and trucks and buses in a long line. The people inside the cars look either angry or sleeping."

"He has a sense of humor."

"Max is my honey."

"When are you going home?"

"I don't know. When Willem finishes."

"…so, business?"

"He has family here, an uncle." Eloise hesitates a second or two before she says, "The uncle had a stroke, so Willem looks after him."

"That's very nice."

"I don't know if it's nice, really. The uncle is also very rich. How, I don't know. Willem doesn't tell me much. We're supposed to be in the will – or Willem is."

"Well lucky Willem."

"I'm just homesick for Max."

It sounds like you'll be rich, too."

"Or that's what the uncle *says*. Who knows, really? I sometimes think the uncle tells Willem these things to get him to stay." Eloise does not look at me but she pauses, takes a breath and says, "What about you? Business, pleasure, what?"

"More business than pleasure."

The girl is a talker, far more than me. I can see why her husband keeps things to himself. I am more like Willem. There is no need for me to go into Theresienstadt and the Colonel with her. If my trip was just for pleasure, there are easier places to find it than Morocco. Not that Tangier isn't charming but there are other ports that charm and do not take me this far from my home.

I look at Eloise, finally. It isn't a long look. I turn back to the ocean. Big waves with whitecaps roll-in, one after the other. The energy of the Atlantic is frightening to me. It's an enormous thing, its fierceness, its indifference. The ocean does not know you and it does not want to know you. You can float in it and swim in it and disappear inside of it.

There is a bruise on the side of Eloise's right eye, a discoloration. It's purple and green like the ones on her wrist. She wears the sunglasses to hide the bruise. There could be other bruises.

Most women are ambivalent about telling the ones who care for them how they were hurt and who hurt them. If they do want to talk, they do not know how to begin the talk and they do not want others to think they have chosen this or that man stupidly. In this culture, the wives and the girlfriends wear heavy makeup and dark glasses to hide the marks and they will glance away instead of looking at you. Women of more primitive cultures will use mud to hide the bruises and talk about spirits attacking them in their dreams.

Eloise is nodding her head to another new song. Her fingertips tap on the radio next to her. She mumbles the words and hums the parts when she does not know the words. This is a song I like, too. "The Best Thing That Ever Happened to Me." Gladys Knight and the somebodies. I am not sure who the somebodies are but they are very good. Eloise is also drawing a circle in the sand with a bare toe.

"Where did you get the bruises on your face?" I am looking at the ocean when I say this.

"I'm sorry, what?"

"...your face."

"You mean my makeup? What do you mean?"

"Who did that to you?" I won't let her off the hook.

"Did what?" She follows this with, "...nobody."

"So, I'm wrong?"

"Nobody did anything." There is anxiety in her voice.

"Am I wrong?"

"...please don't do this."

"My bet is on Willem."

"It's not what you think."

"Oh? And what do I think?" I already know what Eloise will say.

"That my husband hit me, or whatever."

"What would you call it?"

"Well I wouldn't call it that."

"Then give it a name."

"I fell," Eloise says but the words are not sincere. Her bare toes are wedged under the sand. "I am a clumsy person. Ask Willem. We are always joking about it. I once fell and hit the corner of a dining room chair and lost a tooth, a molar. We couldn't believe it. The tooth broke at the root."

Last year a friend was beaten by her husband. I chose not to say anything because I did not want her to get upset and leave our friendship. I was afraid I would lose her and I do not have that many friends. Four days later the husband broke her right arm and shattered her hand with a ball-peen hammer.

I have learned not to wait.

"Where are the other bruises?" I say and I stop looking at the ocean and look at Eloise. Her shoulders and her lips have a tremor. Her dark glasses show the last of a pink and orange sky. "Some beaters are very considerate," I tell her. "They will only hit the parts you can cover up, the back, the stomach, the chest. Is that what Willem does? Does he think he's doing you a favor? Does he say, 'See,

darling, I love you too much to embarrass you'?
They love to say that, how they love you too much.
'See what you made me do,' they'll say. If only you'd
change your attitude everything would be all right."

Eloise stands, her back to me, her radio off and
tucked under her arm.

"We love each other," she says.

"There are better ways to love."

"You don't know things."

"Yes, I do. I know things very well."

"He can be a kind person."

"But not as often as you'd like."

Eloise is walking away from me. Her free hand
is holding the ends of her blond hair to keep the
wind from getting to it.

"You can come see me," I say. But I do not go
after her. I brush the sand from the back of my skirt.
"Day or night," I say. "I am in the Villa de France
like you, the same floor. My name is Liora. As she
gets further from me I call out to her, "I can help
you, Eloise. You'll need a friend and I can be that
friend for you."

SIX

THERE IS A WHITE MARBLE fireplace in Dalal's hotel sitting room. A floor to ceiling mirror begins on both sides of the fireplace and rises above and about it like one of the old keyhole shaped doors in the Medina. Very Moroccan, very dramatic. A fat brass clock and white and blue porcelain vases are on the mantle.

I see these things from the doorway.

"What a brave person," Dalal says. Then she covers the beginning of her smile with her fingertips. My friend is wearing a black abaya—a dress that goes the length of her—and her black hijab. Perhaps she has dressed up for this occasion. "I have made us some mint tea," she says. "Not as good as the Café Hafa but good enough. We will have mint tea and some fortune telling, what could be a better evening, yes?"

"I'm nervous about it," I confess to her. And that is very true. I am still standing in the hallway.

"I will tell you what you tell me," my friend says. "You say, 'I have seen it all before,' isn't that it? Don't you always say, 'Oh, Dalal, people are not all that different from one another'? So, I say to you, I have seen it all before as well. We are more alike than different." She extends her open hand toward the sitting room to invite me in. "This is my safe place."

The sofa and chairs are muted green and the walls are also green but two shades lighter. There is a large painting above the sofa. It's a forest with rabbits, deer and foxes. The animals are primitive looking and they hide amid trees and large red and yellow tulips.

"I will go get our tea," Dalal says. She is already heading to the shadowy corner of the room where a small pot rests on what must be an electric hot plate. "You sit and think about a question you'd like to ask the cards."

"I don't have a question."

"Of course you do."

"What do people usually ask?"

I am already regretting this.

"I do not interfere with that."

"You sound like me," I say.

"See. What did I tell you?"

I know I am anxious but I also know anxiety will only give me the trouble I offer it. And this night is for my friend Dalal.

I must remind myself that Dalal is one of the good people. When she talks to me I feel I have known her forever. But it's more than that. Yesterday, as we were walking from the Café Hafa, we saw a small thin girl leaning against the café wall and sobbing. She could not have been more than five or six. Dalal had knelt in front of her and spoke to her in Arabic and brushed the hair from the child's forehead. I'd watched the two of them become friends and it did not take very long. The girl had been separated from her mother and Dalal and I stayed with the child for maybe ten or fifteen minutes. The mother returned, very apologetic, very relieved to see her child.

That is my new friend.

Dalal and I are now sitting across from each other, a glass and mahogany coffee table between us. A small white linen cloth is on the table. We're drinking our mint tea and talking about what we should expect from one another during the fortune telling. I'm expected to say my question out loud while I shuffle the cards gently, cards over cards, no poker shuffles and no fancy stuff. Dalal will then lay ten of the cards on the table in a pattern called

The Celtic Cross. All cards will be face down. She
is supposed to turn one up at a time and explain
it. After that, she will talk about the relationships
between my cards. I will decide what all of it means
and I can share that with her or keep it to myself.

"I should have wine for you," Dalal says.

"You should have vodka for me."

"I had a martini once." She is grinning.

"Did you like it?"

"Very much. I felt sinful for a week."

What Dalal and I are doing now is so reminiscent
of my year with Miss Reba, the rituals of the tea,
the gentle shuffle and laying out of the cards, Dalal's
calming manner. The fortune telling itself does not
bother me. I do not believe in fortune telling and I've
told Dalal that. There is tomorrow and tomorrow
but there is no seeing it. We do not get a peek. Never.
That's the rule. It's the ritual and not the fortune
telling that brings Miss Reba back to me. But I know
better than to confuse the two women. I need to keep
them separate in my mind. Dalal is a mother who has
a son and she was once a wife who had a husband.
She is an "ordinary" person in the finest sense of the
word. Miss Reba is none of that.

I REMEMBER REBA sitting cross-legged beside me

on the stone steps of my hut. Sunlight and the aya-huasca smoke from her pipe surrounded us. She wore a Quechuan hat with a bright red feather in the brim.

"I do not think of myself as a frightening person," Reba says.

"You are to me."

"Always that?"

"No, not always. Not like at first."

This was after a couple of months of talking to her and witnessing her caring nature.

Curanderas have been in the world for tens of thousands of years. It is the world's oldest profession, older than prostitution. Curanderas are seen by most cultures as heroes on a heroic journey. These people begin life in an ordinary way, much like Dalal or myself. But early in her life there will be an awakening, what some say is a "call to adventure" and what the clinical among us call a "transient psychotic episode." Here a teacher is sought. The teacher might be a spirit from inside the person or a teacher in the real world. Who or what does the teaching is up to the seeker. The adventure is finished when an internal change has been experienced. The change can happen in many ways and it has many names, salvation, *ruach hakodesh*, satori, enlightenment, death and rebirth, *moksha, fana,* and so on. Call it what you want but all curanderas travel through it and no one can become one without going through it. The road is mandatory. And our person with the once ordinary life will return to his or her group, village, or town transformed. He or she will be become the healer, the teacher, the protector, the gateway to worlds.

Miss Reba became less frightening as I got to know her.

I HAVE BEEN shuffling the fortune telling cards for a minute or so, one card over the next, no fancy stuff. Dalal smiles, nodding her approval. Her face is framed by the black hijab, a very pretty face, round and tanned. She has puffy bow lips and big eyes.

"Now say your question," Dalal tells me.

"Will my business here be successful?" I barely hear myself.

"...what? What was it?"

I have another sip of the mint tea. "Will my business here be successful?" I say, louder this time.

I am grateful I do not have to tell her my business. Talking about the Colonel and Theresienstadt and taking back my life from him is not anything I want to discuss. But the Colonel is the business that brought me to Tangier. That's the only bad thing about my trip. I love the beauty of Tangier, the cafés and the ancient streets, the ocean, the beaches with their umbrella pines. Even the wind taking the sand has a romance to it.

The tea and the cards again bring Miss Reba to mind, that ritual exactness. All anthropology students who do what I do will get a lecture from his or her advisor about the lure of the shaman and shamanism and the need to hold onto science and objectivity.

Fortune telling is less dramatic work. But knocking on Dalal's door tonight was a big deal for me. I am inclined to keep a distance from others but the older I get, the faster my life goes and I do not want to squander what is left of it by sitting alone in a room.

Dalal lays out the first card. Then she lays a second card horizontally over the first card. Cards are also placed above and below and to the right and to the left of the first card.

"This our Celtic Cross," Dalal says.

She has also arranged four additional cards in a vertical line to the right of the cross. These four are like a Greek chorus. They are there to comment on the other cards.

All cards face down.

"Do I concentrate on my question?" Always the good student, it's one of my many curses.

"No. You'll remember," Dalal says

"But what if I don't?"

"The unconscious does not forget, yes?"

Ah. Dalal the therapist.

MISS REBA WILL not go away tonight. I am looking at Dalal's cards but in my mind, I am sitting on the stone steps of my hut. I smell the caapi smoke. The sunshine is white enough to hold my hand to my brow. I cannot help inhaling the smoke, and the muscles in my arms and legs and stomach are loose and drippy the way plastic sinks into a hot radiator. That day the caapi smelled like cigars. I remember talking to her about that, the tobacco scent.

"You've asked me this before," Miss Reba says and took the pipe from her mouth and looked down at the smoking bowl and sniffed it. Then she hooked the pipe back into the right corner of her mouth. "Do you recall? You asked me four or five times. Do you remember asking if I smoked cigars?"

"I've never asked you that."

"Who else smoked cigars?"

"My father doesn't smoke," I say.

"All right, fine. Who else?"

"I don't know. Michael never smoked cigars."

"This is what you do," Miss Reba says. She sighed and looked up at the sky. That day the air was clear and blue and very bright. There was wind coming off the mountains, too. I heard it going through the ruins. Reba says, "You tell me everybody you know who does not smoke a cigar. I said to you, 'Didn't you tell me there was a colonel in the prison camp who smoked cigars?' Which you did tell me, quite a few times. And what do you say?"

THIS IS WHEN Dalal begins tapping her forefinger on the first card. She is looking at the card and the more her finger taps the card the more I come back to her and the fortune telling.

"This represents right now," she says and offers me the card to examine. I look at it but I let her hold it. My friend smiles at me and her teeth are very even and white. "The cards never bite," she says.

"I'm being irrational, I know."

"The card is your current situation."

"What's it called?" It is difficult to stay focused.

"The Ten of Wands."

This card has a picture of a person carrying ten large wands on his or her back. I am not sure if this person carrying the wands is a woman or a man. It's night time and clouds are under a half moon. The face has shadow and the figure wears a long cloak, maybe a cape. What I see is the struggle. The wands weigh heavy, the figure is stooped. I imagine that if the clouds did not cover the moon I would also see that struggle in the person's face.

"Tell me about the picture," Dalal says.

"It's too dark, really."

"A few things can be seen."

I give Dalal a quick-frozen smile. "I'm sorry, this card isn't what I want to think about," I say. "I know I am supposed to look at them and talk about them and tell you what comes to my mind. But what if what goes on in my mind isn't something I want to share?"

"Then you shouldn't do it."

"Don't think badly of me."

"This is supposed to be fun," Dalal says and places her hand on my arm. I feel the warmth of her palm through the sleeve of my blouse. She says, "If it is not fun, no one should have to do it."

We have tests in anthropology. We show the people pictures of ambiguous situations. A man and a woman may or may not be arguing. A boy is holding a toy to his chest and one child is smiling at the boy and another child is looking at the boy and crying. A woman lays in a bed alone and a man is sitting on the edge of the bed with his back to her.

Tell me a story, we ask the person.

What does this picture mean to you?

What are these people thinking and saying?

What happens next?

The window is open in Dalal's hotel room. It's night and the wind from the beach comes into the room cool and damp and with the smell of the ocean. Far away people talk and laugh. I hear flutes and drums and syncopated clapping. The fast is done for another day and the Moroccans have setup tables in the Grand Socco. They are feeding in the night, a bowl of Harira, a glass of milk, perhaps some dates. Candles waver across the gritty sides of old buildings.

"Let me tell you about this card." If a voice could tiptoe in the dark, that would be Dalal's voice now. My friend whispers, "Let me tell you what your card says. 'You may feel weary,' it says. 'You also may be feeling overwhelmed and stressed by your responsibilities,' it says. One more thing, 'Your project, your business. It seemed a good idea at the time but it does not seem like a good idea anymore.' This is what the card is saying."

"That's a lot to say."

"Are you all right?"

"It's a lot to say, isn't it? For one card?"

"Shall we go on? You are not looking very good."

"No, no. Go on."

"The next card is what people call the 'influence' card. It's what might help or challenge you.

The position two card." Dalal turns the card over and studies it without a change in her expression. "All right, this is not bad. What we have is the Five of Cups." There is a picture of a knight with his head bowed. Only two of the five cups are upright. These cups are behind him, out of his sight. "Do you want to look at the picture and tell me what comes to your mind?"

"…I, no. No, you tell me."

"But I cannot know, Liora. You must tell what comes to mind. The specifics are from your life, your situation. I would not know that."

"But you know the general picture, yes?"

"I can do that. But I would advise you to let your mind open to the cards. It's always better, more personal."

"The general idea is fine."

"It's a disappointment," Dalal says. She is hesitant, as if not wanting to bring me the bad news. "Others may have let you down. Or will let you down. The betrayal of a lover perhaps, or a friend. Perhaps something you have been counting on doesn't happen. Or happen the way you want it to. This is difficult to discuss without knowing what you think or feel about the card."

I feel my throat constricting and there is something wrong with my hearing. The flutes and the drums and the syncopated clapping outside the hotel window are gone. The outside talk and laughter have gone, too. All of it has disappeared. I cannot find enough air. I tell myself to relax, breathe in and relax. I inhale but I do not feel the air enter my lungs.

"…Liora?" I hear the concern in Dalal's voice.

"I am all right."

I must be scaring Dalal half to death but I cannot reassure her while I am having an anxiety attack. And I know that's what this is and I know how bad it can get, I have had them before.

"We can do this another time," Dalal says.

I do not argue with her. I tell Dalal I am sorry, so very sorry and I rush out of her hotel suite and shut the door behind me. Light from small lamps on the walls break the darkness with circles of yellow light. I lean against the door and try to get my breath. My stomach is knotted tight and I can hear and feel my pulse in my ears.

WHEN I SHUT my eyes, I hear Miss Reba blowing the ayahuasca smoke up into the air. The blue tint of the smoke goes white in the sunshine. It whirls about and drifts over me. I take a full breath and release it. I do it a second time and a third. The air is chilled and stings the back of my throat.

I am sitting on the stone steps in front of my small hut, its two windows, its turquoise door. Or I am in the memory of being there. Miss Reba is sitting to my left. She has been waiting for me to speak. I turn my head to her but sunlight and smoke conceal her.

"Do you recall talking about this colonel?" Reba says.

"No. Yes, vaguely." Now I want her to leave me alone.

"The colonel at Theresienstadt. He smoked cigars."

"Colonel Kohler."

"Him, exactly. Yes." Miss Reba says this and nods. Her arms are folded against her chest. A thumb and thick forefinger steady the bowl of the pipe. The smell of the ayahuasca smoke has gone from smelling like a cigar to smelling like burning leaves. She says, "Have you noticed how little you talk about your time at Theresienstadt? I know it's difficult to discuss but I wanted to bring this to your attention."

"I am in denial."

"...very much so."

"It's a joke."

"Not to me, it isn't. Not to you, either."

"I'm joking," I say. "You have no sense of humor."

"Theresienstadt was a joke?"

"Of course not. Nobody's saying—"

"Did other people in Theresienstadt see it as a joke?"

"No. Nobody saw it as a joke."

"Good. This is your life. Let's be serious."

What do I say to that?

"Colonel Kohler was there with you," Miss Reba says. She takes the pipe from her mouth and studies the orange ash in the bowl. Reba uses her little finger to tap at the ash. Again, she sucks on the stem and smoke rushes from her nostrils and into the sunny sky. "He was in Theresienstadt. Didn't he smoke a cigar?"

"…no…yes." I remember the colonel. An image of him would come to mind off and on, though never with any consistency.

He was a slender man and taller than my father, who I thought was very tall. The colonel wore round rimless glasses. His uniform always smelled of starch and tobacco. The jacket and the pants had creases down the arms and the legs. I also remember his boots were black and had a good shine.

"What's his name?" Miss Reba is testing me.

"Colonel Smiley." That is what I had called him.

"His real name."

"I was a child."

"You just mentioned his name."

"Give me a second," I say.

"Take your time. It's not a school test."

I had a difficulty with the man's name. I do not know why. One minute I knew the name and the next minute I didn't know the name. I knew his real name but it was easier for me to call him by the name I had made up for him than to call him by what he called himself.

"…Kohler," I say. "K.P. Kohler."

"He was a cigar smoker." It is a statement.

"Yes," I say. "He smoked thin black cigars."

"Your memory has come to you."

"Oh, I am full of surprises."

"But will the memory stay?"

"He was Colonel Smiley to me."

"Today you are the jokester," Miss Reba says. But she is not amused. The hem of her cotton pollera skirt quivers in the wind. I can see it in my peripheral vision. "I am not against a good joke," she says. "But forgive me, I do not understand how you think your stay in Theresienstadt was funny."

"Perhaps I exaggerated."

"You're very clever. I can see you becoming a good anthropologist. Maybe even a very good anthropologist."

"I hear a 'but' in this. But what?"

"You have many ways to avoid what you need to know."

"Doesn't everybody?"

"We're not talking about everybody."

"Some did not get through Theresienstadt," I say.

"I am asking you to be more than brave."

"Joking is a way to get by."

"In the old days, I liked going to the movies," Miss Reba says. "I liked the comedies. I liked to laugh." She stood up and stretched her back and took a deep breath of the cool air. I knew she was done with our talk. Miss Reba was right. I worshiped her the way only a graduate student can adore someone who is seen as wise. "I enjoyed Laurel and Hardy," she tells me. "I liked that man who never smiled, what's-his-name, Buster Keaton. Very funny, very amusing. They showed us our short comings, our lives, our humanity. They were worthy of the laughter we gave them. But you are amused in the wrong places. You are off key. What is the saying? You laugh to keep from crying."

"You can be very cruel."

"Isn't that my job?"

I did not answer.

"One day it will come back to you," Miss Reba says. "This K.P. Kohler, Theresienstadt, what you and your parents endured, it will come back. What you yourself survived. It's always best to keep these things in the daylight."

I left Miss Reba and my field work in June of 1959. That was sixteen years ago. I feel more now and know more about myself. Before I left her, Miss Reba told me to embrace the memories that frighten me. "Find them and pull them into the present," she'd said. "Yesterday looks different in the present."

I know it will be done soon. Leon Nauman has assured me. "We'll take care of everything," he says. "You go to Tangier, hon. Trust me. We may not have the exact street address but we have the location."

SEVEN

THE "MELLAH" WAS WHAT MOROCCANS called the Jewish quarter, very much like a European ghetto. Dalal tells me *mellah* is Arabic for salted, cursed ground. "No crops will grow on salted ground," was the saying. And the same, I suppose, some hoped for the Jews. There were mellahs in the cities of Fes, Rabat, Mogador but none in Tangier or nothing so formal. Dalal says Tangier was one of the few cities in Morocco that accepted different religions and ways of living.

The ghettos were built near the royal palace or the Governor's home. Jews helped strengthen the local economy. Those who ruled the cities wanted the Jews close at hand and protected them. Jewish homes in the Medina were very lovely, and the Jews who lived there usually hosted parties and dinners for the diplomatic crowd.

This morning I am sitting inside *La Synagogue Moise Nahon de Tanger*. It's in the Medina on the Rue des Synagogues. The street is narrow and cut with shadow and sun. Dark double doors are the only marker to the Nahon Synagogue. Once there were seventeen synagogues in the Medina, many Jews, many prayers. Then in 1948 much of the Jewish community either migrated to Israel or traded the Medina for uptown high rises.

I am seated in the back pew. I have not prayed in a long time and I cannot remember the last time. I do not think I have ever prayed as an adult. When I was a girl, my father would take me to shul and I would pray with him but that was to please my father.

WHAT I REMEMBER are the prisoners in Theresienstadt who prayed on their knees beside their bunks and in the lavatories by the long row of white sinks and the ones who prayed outside with their knees in the mud and the dirt. In those days, people prayed everywhere.

If a guard caught a prisoner praying during work the guard would throw the prisoner to the ground and kill him or her with their own shovel.

Or the guard would shoot the prisoner in the head. It depended on how hot the day was and how much work the guard had to do.

Theresienstadt was an in-between place. A place that lead to other places, a waystation. It was not a ghetto or a concentration camp but thirty-three thousand Jews died there.

The Nazis called it "spa town" where old Jews could retire and not have to work in the labor camps. That was what they said to the German people. And it had a half truth to it, a twisted and weak truth. Theresienstadt was a place for Nazi deception, their kindest face, their attempt at public relations. Theresienstadt had a swimming pool but no one ever swam in it. The pool was filled only when important guests came to visit. Guests included the Red Cross, newspaper people, diplomats and other dignitaries, so on and so on. There was a lending library of sixty thousand books but I do not remember anyone reading. Jewish artists from Germany, Czechoslovakia and Austria were sent to Theresienstadt. Musicians, professors and writers were there, too. These extraordinary men and women gave us lectures, performances, concerts. All that was true and we were very thankful for them.

Thinking about it years later, I am stunned at the madness of it. We were given luxuries only when important guests visited. There were stores in the camp that displayed baked goods and meats. My father had medicines to treat his patients during these visits. But after the Red Cross left and the newspaper people and the diplomats had gone, the baked goods and the meats and the medicines were taken from us. The shops were like scenery on a movie set and remained empty until the next tour of the camp.

In our everyday lives, we did not have enough to eat and what food we did have was old and spoiled. We were forever too cold or too hot and the buildings smelled of shit and piss and there was no sanitation. The Nazis knew these things would kill the sick ones, the old ones.

Let's not forget another truth. This place was a deportation camp for the killing centers in eastern Europe.

I was one of fifteen thousand children who passed through Theresienstadt between November 1941 and the middle of 1945. We painted pictures and wrote poetry about our lives in the camp, what we saw, what we dreamed, what we felt. We did this in secret. Encouraged by the musicians, the artists and the professors, we talked about the things that frightened us, how the people we loved had died or were dying.

Ninety percent of us died, too.

There was no stopping it.

The old Jews and the young Jews prayed when no guard was looking. They prayed in the morning and in the night. I could not turn this way or that without seeing a Jew in prayer. The other prisoners had to pick them up from the ground and the bathrooms and the living areas. We had to tell them that the journalists and the camera people would be there soon and if they did not go about their lives and stop the praying they'd be deported to the killing camps in the east.

"You do not know how good you have it," the Nazis liked to tell us. "You should be thankful for having it so good. A swimming pool, a library, wonderful conversations with interesting people. You should thank each soldier here that grandpapa and grandmamma will live out their lives in comfort."

At the height of it, the Nazis were killing between twenty to fifty thousand a day in the camps to the east. They did not want old people taking up space on the trains.

I AM SITTING in the back pew of *La Synagogue Moise Nahon de Tanger*, indulging myself, recalling my life. I am sure being here this morning has to do with my business in Tangier and last night's fortune telling with my friend Dalal. I apologized to her earlier in the morning but she would have none of it. We seem to meet our best friends by circumstance. I am grateful she is who she is, that she can roll with the punches, so-to-speak.

I do not know how to go about praying, how to even start. Do I apologize first? Do I say, "I'm sorry I have not talked to you, dear Lord?" Do I dismiss my reasons before they are dismissed for me? Maybe I should discuss the franticness of my days and my hope for compassion? Does the Lord know that I prayed as a girl simply to please my daddy, to see him look down on me and smile? What child in her right mind would not do that? Or should I be courageous and tell the truth, the absolute truth, nothing but the truth: I did not believe in God when I was a girl and I do not believe in God now that I am a woman. More than that, I think the people who pray to this or that God cannot bear to think they are less than a speck of star dust in a disinterested and unforgiving universe.

But now I am thinking maybe they are right, or might be right, those Jews on their knees, those Jews who prayed any place, any time.

Who else will listen, after all?

Who else will hear me?

I look about the room, this ancient place, this hidden place. I need to be here in Nahon

Synagogue with its polished white and black marble floor and its columns and arches. Gleaming chandeliers crisscross the high ceiling. The walls are flecks in worn gold wallpaper. There is a stale smell, the smell of wood and the ocean and the hot afternoons given to matters of the spirit. It is a good-sized room and I can see the second floor where the wives and mothers and daughters would sit and pray and watch the men *daven* below them, men who rocked back and forth to the kaddish, men who were mystified by their women and the blood of their women.

I'M ALSO THINKING of the Colonel.

"Well look at you," K.P. Kohler liked to say, the man I'd always thought of as Colonel Smiley. "Oh, we are going to be wonderful friends. You are *very* lovely. Did you know that, darling? Do you have any idea how lovely you are?"

That's how he would talk.

Or he would stop talking and just walk around me and look. It was like an inspection. When he walked, he made sounds like he wanted to clear his throat but he never did.

"Lovely legs, lovely everything," the Colonel would say. "But I suppose you don't care about that. Maybe you don't even know. Now those little blond girls know they are beauties, don't they? They love to prance and flirt. Twitch their parts. Isn't that the expression? But not the ones like you. No, no, not the dark ones with eyes like that, not the ones like you. Tell me, darling, where did you learn English?"

"My daddy."

"Your poppy, how delightful."

"No, no. It's 'daddy,' not 'poppy.' If you speak English, you say 'daddy.' Everybody knows that."

The Colonel always talked in English with me. He enjoyed the practice, I think. After he would walk around me he'd sit on the Victorian couch that was in the corner of his office. He wore a starched tan uniform. His legs were long and thin and crossed at the knee. The Colonel also had on his rimless glasses. And he smelled of lilac cologne and his cigars. He sometimes patted the couch for me to sit beside him.

This particular afternoon was hot and the sunlight went through the open windows with a yellow brilliance and covered my lap in a dusty buttercup color.

"My daddy is a good teacher."

"An intelligent Jew," the Colonel said. He touched the back of my hair with his fingers. "I am the first to say this."

When he touched me, my shoulders quivered and I felt my skin go hot on my neck and chest. I liked the feeling but it scared me and I also did *not* like it. Or perhaps I liked it too much but I didn't know what the feeling was or what I was supposed to do with it.

"We are going to America." I barely got the words out.

"America," the Colonel said. "From sea to shining sea. Joan Crawford and Ray Milland. Hot dogs and the Dodgers." He grinned and his teeth were big and even and white. "Not too soon, I hope. How dreadful for me if you were to go too soon. What would I do? How would your poor Colonel get by? I'd be a crushed and empty shell."

"Daddy said very soon. Maybe tomorrow."

"No, darling. I do not think you will go tomorrow."

"You don't know that. We will go when we want to."

This had made him laugh. I always amused him.

"…when we want to," I said again. I did not like him laughing. I did not like him thinking he knew everything.

"That is a shame," the Colonel said and turned his face into a sad face but could not quite rid himself of his smile. Then he sighed as if he were terribly disappointed. "What will I do with the lovely new dress I got for a certain pretty girl? New shoes, too. Patent leather shoes with bows. What shall I do, what other pretty girl shall I find? Now I will have to find another pretty girl."

"You didn't get me a dress." I heard the hope in my voice.

"Who didn't?"

"…you."

"I said I would get you a dress, did I not?"

"So find another pretty girl."

"Suppose I do not want another pretty girl?"

"Then I do not know what to tell you." The same heated feeling came to the back of my neck and my stomach. And the air seemed too thick to breathe.

I was thirteen years old and once in a while I was scared but most of the time I was too dense to be scared. I think he enjoyed all that. My Colonel Smiley, my… what? My suitor? Ha! Yes, I believe he was courting me. And I believe I knew it. I think he liked my sassiness, my adolescent bravado. Of course, I saw him as very old and very foolish but now I know he was in his thirties, thirty-two, thirty-three, not old in the scheme of things. God knows he was anything but foolish.

It amazes me how my history can appear with such detail, how one thing ignites another. I am forever surprised at what I carry around.

❖ ❖ ❖

THERE IS A large skylight in Nahon Synagogue and the skylight is open and the late morning sun is warm on my hands and my face and it also brings a breeze and the sounds of the Medina. The sun reflects off the wood pews and the marble floor. Last time I visited a synagogue I was nine or ten and my father was intent on me learning about what he called my heritage. I cared nothing about this, of course, synagogues were for old men in tallises and brown or gray felt hats, but I adored my father. And I still do.

Amazing. My talk with the Colonel Kohler has not left me.

"Keep your presents," I'd told him.

"How cruel you are," the Colonel said and placed the flat of his hand over his heart and looked at me. He did have a second face, a sad face, his mouth turned down, his eyes shiny with vague tears. Yet with it all, he still looked amused. Sunlight from the window flashed across the lenses of his rimmed glasses. "I must let this be my lesson," he had said. Whispered it dramatically to himself. "This is what happens when people love too deeply, Liora. Oh, it's true. This is how we get ourselves wounded. But better to have loved and lost, as they say."

Colonel Kohler stood and stretched his back and walked over to the closet by the metal filing cabinets. He opened the door and retrieved a white dress with lavender flowers and a crinoline beneath it.

"And what would this be?" the Colonel said. He rubbed the hem between his slender thumb and forefinger. His fingers were delicate and long and his nails were manicured. "Silk, I think. I believe this is silk. Yes, a person of taste can tell by the feel of it. Would you care to feel it?"

"No thank you."

"Oh come, come." He stretched his arm toward me and gave the hanger a jiggle and the dress trembled and fluttered.

"No," I said. I said it very firmly. "No is what I mean. N. O. Do you understand N. O.?"

"You're very sure, aren't you?"

"Completely sure."

"I don't think so, my darling."

"Think again," I said.

"This is a special dress," Colonel Kohler said. "This dress was made in Paris. It's a dress rich papas buy their very beautiful and good girls." The Colonel smiled at the dress, admiring it, and showed his big white teeth. He held the dress up and brushed the wrinkles from it with his free hand. "Beautiful French girls dream of wearing such a dress."

"You don't know what I like."

"Oh, I know you," the Colonel said. "Don't I? Don't I know you? Oh, you know I do." He smiled one of his enormous smiles. "Let me tell you what you are thinking," he said. "You are thinking, 'How lovely I would look in that silk dress my Colonel bought me. How gorgeous. I would become a beautiful Parisian girl in that dress and show off my slim wonderful legs and all the Parisian boys would watch me and wish madly they could know me and be my friend.' Isn't that it? Isn't that what you are thinking? How lovely you'd look, how beautiful? And you would be right."

"Being lovely is not everything."

"…little patent leather shoes."

"I do not want to hear it," I said.

"Let me show you the shoes."

"No thank you. N. O." I remember pressing my hands to my ears.

"How resolved you are, darling."

I had wanted to feel that dress and wear that dress more than I wanted to breathe air. I wanted to put it on and go back to Prague and show all my friends, particularly that hateful girl Dorota and her snooty friends. I wanted my fingertips to run the length of it, the lavender flowers, the crinolines. I wanted to gather the thick silk material between my fingers and press it to my face and feel it touch my cheek and inhale the scent of it.

Inhale Paris. Inhale rich papas.

Inhale all those imaginary French girls and boys.

I AM SITTING in the back wood pew of *La Synagogue Nahon de Tanger* and thinking about all of this, the lavender dress Colonel K.P. Kohler had bought for me in Paris, the patent leather shoes. But more than these gifts, I recall the desperate feeling I had about Mother and Father and me being trapped in a place that gave no thought to our welfare, to our lives. We were treated as less than human then and we were treated that way for days and weeks and months and we had to fight with the feeling to see ourselves that way. That was why I liked the Colonel, at least at the start of it.

I'd become special again.

Sunshine is intense on the walls of the Synagogue, its worn gold flecked wallpaper. Marble columns are showing the sun. Sand and dust have come down from the open skylight and lay scattered about the floor and the dark pews and the mahogany and red velvet lectern. The lectern is not in front of the pews but to the left side of them. Perhaps the Jews had a lot to pray about and did not have time to look at the rabbi.

❖ ❖ ❖

COLONEL K.P. KOHLER admired my English and he admired my father for teaching me English.

"He speaks better than an American," I'd said.

"I would not doubt it, darling."

"He could be an American right away."

"If it's his wish, so be it." The first time the Colonel had talked to me had been outside the ochre colored building that was his office. I was very impressed by his starched uniform, his rimless glasses, the neatness of the man. When he stood and talked, his hands were folded behind him. "America, America," he said. It was an exaggerated wistfulness.

I learned English at school in Prague but I also learned it from my father. He always talked about our family going to America and he used to tell me, "The better you know the language the better you will fit in, Liora." My father and mother and I would speak English during breakfast and dinner. Father was our self-elected tutor. "Please pass me the bread," Mother would say in English. Or, "Is not the chicken tender and plump?" My father liked to say, "We should all pretend we are having a good time. One day we will be happy we did this." My English included the sentence, "Thank you for passing the potatoes." And also, "What delicious meats."

The question mother and I most dreaded from Daddy was, "Tell me about your day?" This required a recount of our entire day in English and nobody but Daddy enjoyed doing that. Mother and I learned how to say, "You do not want to know." Or, "So-so," with a wiggle of our hand. Or, "Our day today was just like yesterday." My father did not get angry but he was not happy. "Do you think you can get away with that in America?" he'd shake his head and say. "Do you think that is what Americans do? Just wiggle their hands and say, 'so-so?' "

EIGHT

THE IDEA OF LEON NAUMAN is always better than actually hearing from him. I am already getting annoyed and anxious. I do not need Leon telling me, "We may not have the exact street address but we have the location." What does that *mean*? There are many things I do not need right now. I do not need Tangier to become another Costa Rica or Geneva. I do not need to chase Colonel Kohler half around the world only to end up with jet lag and an empty wallet. I do not need to lose what hope I have left.

And I do not need to hear, "What are you wearing, Doc?"

"Where are you?"

"London. What you wearing?"

"I know you think that's funny, Leon. But if I didn't laugh the first time, I won't be laughing the second time."

"Develop a sense of humor," he says.

"Both of us."

Leon Nauman is a stoop shouldered little man in his late sixties and an old friend of my father's. Leon is a very good investigator, my father believes one of the best in the business, but the man flirts like a vaudeville comedian. I do not know if I should be amused or insulted.

The phone is pressed between my ear and my raised shoulder. I am in the room at the *Villa de France* and gently filing a split cuticle on my little finger. I've been looking out the window past the *Rue de la Liberté* and toward St. Andrew with its white minaret looking bell tower.

"Is the job done?" I want to know. "Or are you just calling me to say something you'll regret later in the day?"

"...Jesus." This is followed with a weary breath.

"Oh, I'm sorry. Did I hurt your sensibilities?"

"Don't bust balls, Liora."

"Dr. Womack," I say and hold the cuticle I have been working on toward the window, the sunlight. It still doesn't look right. "And I am *not* concerned with your balls, Leon."

"You and everybody else."

"*Or* your sex life, Leon."

"Also, you and everybody else."

"Let's keep the sparkling personality in check, Leon. Okay? You're talking to your employer."

"I'm a dear friend of your father's."

"No discounts," I say.

"Fine. The job is finished and it's not finished."

"Do not get cryptic on me, Leon. I'm not in the mood for cryptic."

"Tangier is the right place. Okay? It's definitely the right place. I'll discuss the rest of it when I see you."

"Discuss it now."

"Not on the phone."

"All right. When will you be in Tangier?"

"Tomorrow. In the evening." His voice has gone from forced friendly to annoyed. "But Air Tangier is *farkacta*. You know *farkacta*?"

"Yes, I know *farkacta*." It's Yiddish for fucked up. Roughly translated.

"I got a flight at six," Leon's saying. "I could be there at eight. I could be there at nine. It could be midnight on a Tuesday. Or with my luck, next week. Understand what I'm saying? Who knows? They don't know, I don't know. It's out of my control. This thing is in God's hands. I'm there when I'm there."

"That's not acceptable."

"It's in God's hands, Liora. Excuse me. Dr. Womack."

"I'm not paying God."

"You're busting balls."

"Get on the plane."

"I can see why you're not married."

"Are you married, Leon? Currently married?" I reach a Leon Nauman threshold faster than Superman can pass a speeding bullet. "How many exes now? I've lost count. Six, seven? What are we talking?"

"…eight."

"Very good. One more and your ex-wives can play the Red Sox."

Two weeks ago, Leon said I needed to fly to Tangier and get a room at the *Villa de France* on the 15th. He said he had other business but he would meet me between the 15th and the 17th. Leon always has other business. It could be in Paris, Barcelona, Disneyland, whatever. It doesn't matter. He is a hunting dog who gets distracted by squirrels. Where his paycheck is coming from is irrelevant to him. He has an attention deficit disorder. It is now the 18th and I am getting this phone call from him and he tells me the job is finished and it's not finished. And I am not supposed to question him about this because we're talking on phones. He's telling me maybe he will be here tonight or maybe he won't. Maybe it'll be next week. Maybe when he runs out of other things to do.

The man irritates me. I know I am not the sweetest person in the world. I know that, I own it. I not only own it but I am comfortable with it. What Leon thinks of me one way or the other is not the quasar in my universe. I mean let's get serious. This isn't who is the Queen of the Hop and who isn't. This is money. This is information. This is I do not care who you are, just tell me what you know and I will pay you. I do not want to be your girlfriend. I do not want to be the woman who flirts with you. I am not interested in being the next ex-wife in your hideous little ballclub. Give me the information I requested and I'll give you the money you need and you can go buy a hamburger with it and leave me alone. Why is that so difficult for Leon Nauman? What else does he need and why does he think I'm supposed to give it to him?

I am a person who knows the cruelties and the shadows and I am not a pushover. I am not a woman who shuts up and gets along.

My father will tell you that, Leon's dear friend.

It's the late morning and the sunlight coming in from the windows of my room at the *Villa de France* is hot and it shines on the white walls and the waxed wood floor. There is also an ocean breeze that does not stop. Tangier reminds me of being in a hot room with a ceiling fan.

Leon is saying, "…this isn't one of your better ideas, Liora—you hiring an investigator. Doing what you're planning to do. When we get together, you and me, we're going to have a heart-to-heart. Go to one of those cafés where you can look at the water. Who doesn't like the Mediterranean? Maybe get some tea. People there, they love tea."

"You sure the guy is here?"

"What did I say?"

"Let me tell you what you said, Leon. I'll give you an exact quote."

"Why does that not surprise me."

"You said, 'We'll take care of everything.' You said, 'You go to Tangier, hon. Trust me.' You want me to go on?"

"I like the last part, the 'trust me' part. Why don't you do that?"

"It's been twenty-nine years. I'm tired of the search."

"…I know."

"The disappointment is too much," I say.

"I won't let you down. But if this one doesn't do it, if we lose him—"

"I don't want to hear that."

"I'm saying 'if,' alright? *If.* That's not the worst thing. Look, I'm an older man. You live long enough, you get to know things. There are things you walk by. You do not stop, you do not look. You walk by. I may not be an educated individual like you and your father but you should pay attention. That's the most important part of life, to know when to stop and when to walk by. Let's not get into it now. All right, okay? I'm just giving you a what-you-call-it, a heads-up."

"That's very thoughtful, Leon."

"You need a gun? I can get you a gun."

"That's not necessary," I say.

"We'll talk."

"Not about guns, we won't."

"You think this is Norfolk?" Leon says. "You're in Tangier. People think Tangier, they think artsy-fartsy, hashish and queers. But somebody like you, Liora. That's a whole different situation. Somebody in your situation, I'd come prepared."

"I agree. Bring me vodka."

"I can't hear you." The phone line has off and on static.

"Bring Vodka," I say again. Louder, "This isn't the fifties with the Spanish and the French. These people don't drink."

"I'm glad you find your situation amusing."

"I've been in worse."

"You don't know what's involved here."

"That's why I'm waiting on you, Leon."

"Fine. Once I get there I'll get you a gun. I know people."

"I wouldn't know what to do with it," I tell him.

"What's to know? You aim, you shoot."

"That's not what I do."

THAT'S NOT COMPLETELY honest. Colonel Kohler taught me to fire a gun in the camp. He would stand close behind me and put his hand on my waist. I could feel his breath on my cheek, the smell of cigar tobacco and cloves. Things in me got jittery. My cheeks and my shoulders warmed. This was what happened when he got too close. "Remember, you are in charge of the firearm, darling," he'd whisper. He used his other hand to steady my arm and help me aim.

There was a target near the window in his office and the target was round and made of wood and thick fibrous material. He and I practiced firing at its red bullseye. Once a prisoner yelled, "Hey, you got your little girl whore in there?" The Colonel walked over to the open window and fired his pistol into the window of the barracks across the way. I saw a prisoner fall and disappear from view.

The colonel was not the only soldier who did this. Who shot us. Who beat us. Who cut our legs with bayonets when we were not moving fast enough. I suppose it could have been worse. We could have been in one of the death camps being marched through the woods and into the cremos. People could have fashioned jewelry from our bones and lamp shades from our skin. We could have been gassed and burned and thrown into lye pits and into ovens and roasted what remained of us. We were all things but human to them. We were targets. We were pets. Were what the SS doctors experimented on to advance a bizarre science and to eliminate the sludge end of a gene pool.

Until then I hadn't experienced myself as a witness. That was the day I became one. I became the person who does not react, the person who does not protest or interfere.

I said nothing to Colonel Kohler, not in the beginning and not the other times. I watched him fire into the barracks as if I were watching a play. It could not be real. That was what I told myself. There could not be these lives lost. The prisoners across the way had become black and white striped ducks in a shooting gallery. Boom, twirl. Boom, flip, flip. The Colonel smiled when he would shoot at the windows of the barracks but then again, the Colonel always smiled. That did not change.

Shooting prisoners for extra target practice began after Colonel Kohler had ordered the small houses built on the grounds. The prisoners had become more competitive with each other. They wanted to live in these houses. They wanted to have better lives, if only for the day or two the Red Cross and the journalists toured our camp.

They'd become more confrontive with Colonel Kohler, too. I'm guessing it started the day he decided my family would live in one of the houses all the time.

"—Because you are such a darling child," he'd tell me and kiss my forehead. "You make life in this terrible place bearable."

That decision had infuriated the whole camp. But the Colonel was a stubborn man and the more the prisoners made their anger known the more of them he shot until it became a sport to him.

I felt fear in that house. I'd hear the prisoners calling me a whore or calling my mother a whore. But I knew nowhere was safe. I certainly didn't want to go back to the barracks and all that blood on the window and floor. I didn't want to ask, "What is this? What happened here?" Shooting prisoners for extra target practice began after Colonel Kohler had ordered the small houses built on the grounds. I don't know if there was a connection between these two events. But I believe some prisoners became more agitated, more completive, wanting to live in these houses, wanting to have better lives – if only for a day or two when the Red Cross and the journalists toured the camp.

I also believe the prisoners became more con-frontive with the Colonel the day he decided my family would live in one of these houses all the time.

"—Because you are such a darling child," he'd tell me and kiss my forehead. "You make life in this terrible place bearable."

I felt both relief and fear in that house. Is that possible? I could walk into my bedroom and pretend I was somewhere else, somewhere safe. But then I'd hear the prisoners calling me a whore or calling my mother a whore. And I knew nowhere was safe. I didn't want to go back to the barracks, though; I didn't want to see the blood on the window and the blood on the floor. I didn't want to ask, "What is this? What happened here?"

Leon is saying, "I can teach you to fire a gun." He's trying to say this casually but there is an urgency to his talk. "What do you say? No charge, something to make up for my attitude. I am not a bad guy, you know. Not every guy is a bad guy."

"We'll talk. Buy yourself a flask."

"I'm offering my expertise." The static on the phone line is getting worse.

"I don't need a gun, Leon. I need a drink."

"I'm not sure you know what you need."

"You're in London. Go buy a flask and fill it with vodka."

"You think this is a joke."

"No, Leon," I say. "This is not a joke, all right?" Don't go thinking I'm so foolish, you insult me. But things are relative and this is small time, I can tell you that. My life is anti-climactic, what I have been through, what my family has been through. Nothing will ever match that time. Or be that frightening, that dramatic. But it does not mean I ignore serious things. It doesn't mean I don't put things in perspective, not that I expect you to understand."

"Hey, I understand. Of course I understand."

"Oh please. You don't get shit, Leon." I am leaning against the window sill, the phone snug between my shoulder and ear. It's after eleven in the morning and I am still in my terrycloth bathrobe. I have yet to take a shower and put myself together for the day. I am forgetting my morning run, too. I have forfeited the hard, wet sand under my bare feet, the early heat of the sun and the calming silky rush of my endorphins. I am becoming more and more preoccupied since coming to this place. There is a no-clock endlessness to Tangier. The city will sneak up on you and rob you of your senses. The city is unapologetically seductive. Tangier has a one-day-blurring-into-the-next attitude. It takes me in and it lulls me with its ocean and its wind and its sun and I want to disregard my reason for being here. My task. I begin feeling like I have fallen into a rabbit hole even Alice would have admired. I tell Leon, "I've gone unarmed into bigger horrors than this."

"You don't think I know, Liora?"

"Who knows what you know?"

"I also lived in Prague."

"I was too busy to notice," I say.

"I'm aware. Many were too busy."

"Then give me credit."

"This isn't about credit," Leon says. The static remains on the line and often it becomes louder than his words. "Your father and me, we grew up on the river together," he says. "I don't remember a time when he was not my friend. Your family and mine, we come from the same neighborhood. I held you when you were a baby in the crib."

Leon is starting to tell an old story I have heard before but I'll let him go on with it because I like hearing stories about the neighborhood, and this story makes me feel better about him.

"You were a pissy thing, even then," Leon says. "Skinny and cute but very pissy, a real pistol. Your bottom could fit in the palm of my hand. Did I ever tell you that?"

"Many times."

"That's how tiny. Right in my palm."

"Let's not discuss my bottom," I tell him.

"I'm just saying."

"I know what you're saying."

I thought this familiar story might feel calming and give me some peace but today it's turning very creepy. And I start to feel more than uncomfortable. Leon is going to deliver the news I have been waiting to get for years, information that will change my old fantasies into something real. Now I am not sure if I want to know, truly know, maybe the curiosity about it and the fantasies of it are as far as I can go and feel safe.

The thought of my bottom fitting in Leon Nauman's hand at any age is a bad visual.

"What's your point, Leon?"

"I do not need to see you hurt," he says. The static on the phone line has begun to take the ends of his words. "Or worse. And God help us if it's worse. I do not want the responsibility of that, Liora. All right? That's the long and the short, I do not want the responsibility. I do not want anything happening to you because of me."

I keep thinking about what Leon and I talked about earlier.

"But if this one doesn't do it, if we lose him—"

"I don't want to hear that."

"I'm saying 'if,' alright? If. That's not the worst thing. Look, I'm an older man. You live long

enough, you get to know things. There are things you walk by. You do not stop, you do not look. You walk by..."

I am at the window of my hotel room. Tourists are waiting under the ever warming sun to see the inside of St. Andrew's Church. Most of them are in shorts and sneakers or sandals. Some wear baseball caps. Practically all of them have cameras. There is laughter and chatter but I cannot hear what the talk is or why they are laughing.

"Where were you, Leon?" Once again reality of Leon is never as good as thinking about him.

"...What?" His voice has a wariness.

"You heard me. It's a question."

"What do you mean, where was I?"

"When your best friend and his family were kidnapped during the night, when these criminals came into our home and took us off to Theresienstadt, where were you?" I say. "It's not a difficult question, is it? How did you get out of that? How did you outsmart them, what did you do? Who did you betray, who did you turn in?"

"That's unfair, Liora."

"No, it isn't," I tell him. A weight has come over me, the back of my neck, my shoulders. "That is not an unfair question, Leon. Referees will not leap out of the bushes and blow their whistles at us. You know what's true. This is what every Jew who

was ever dragged into Theresienstadt has thought
about every other Jew they did not meet there. How
did you get so lucky?"

NINE

THIS MORNING DALAL AND I met her twelve-year-old son Aabid at the train station and we are all riding back to the *Villa de France* in a taxi that has the odor of kif in it. Aabid is small for his age and has tan fleshy arms and legs. His black hair looks as though it has been sheered recently with an electric razor. He is a serious boy or at least has yet to smile at me or his mother. Maybe he needs time to warm up. Aabid is very neat and wears a white shirt with a subdued tie. He also wears a gray suit that has short pants. His right knee is swollen and bruised a purple and yellow color. At first, he does not say much in the taxi but I catch him glancing at me. Dalal is glad to see him and fusses with what hair he has left from the buzz cut.

She also fusses with his tie and any wrinkles she notices on his suit.

"What a beautiful boy," Dalal says to him and kisses his forehead.

Aabid leans his head away from her.

Boys do not like mothers loving them in front of others.

"What happened to your knee?" I say.

"A classmate pushed me." Ah the boy speaks.

"That's terrible."

"Yes, very terrible," he says. "Very, very terrible, I absolutely agree. The boy is much bigger than me, a huge boy. He plays sports and has big arms and a big neck. And he is two years older. How do I protect myself?"

"So not a friend," I say.

"Khalid?" The boy snorts at the idea. Aabid is looking at the bruise on his puffy tan knee as he talks. "That is a joke, yes? Khalid is a boy in name only. He has no friends. Maybe the lizards and the spiders but that is all."

"I can see why." I nod toward his swollen knee.

"He followed me to the train station this morning and pushed me down and told me I better not come back to Casablanca." Aabid touches the bruise on his knee with the tip of his finger and winces. "I tell him, 'This is my home. I will come back when I feel like it.' And he pushed me again and I fell and hit my knee in the same spot. Can you imagine this? The exact same spot. I truly must be an unfortunate boy. Then I say to Khalid, 'You always think you are so rough and tough. But I have fooled you. I have defeated you. Anybody can beat me,' I say to him. I say, 'Do not deceive yourself into thinking you are such a tough guy because I am on the ground. Smaller boys than you have done that. It is true,' I tell him. 'Boys with smaller arms. Boys that do not play sports or think they are clever.' May even the spiders and the lizards forsake him."

"Good for you," I say.

"You should not defend yourself with such humility," Dalal says. "You are just as good as he is in every way. No, better. You were raised better. I am positive your grades are better. You are a very bright boy."

"Khalid is an honor student."

"I am sure he is not a good one," Dalal says.

THE TAXI HAS no air conditioning and even with the windows rolled down it is still very hot. Dalal bought me a brown hijab for this occasion. "It will make Aabid feel more comfortable," she'd said. Both of us are wearing our hijabs this morning. The hooded covering is a frame for my face and I can feel the sweat on the top of my head and the back of my neck. I look like Katharine Hepburn in *The Lion in Winter* but without her cheekbones.

Women don't have a fair deal here in these pious countries. The men are anxious about women and demand too much from them. The men like to disguise these anxieties in religion. "You should not do this," they say. "You should not do that." The anxiety the men have is the same that men have about women everywhere. It has nothing to do with religion and everything to do with other men. The men think, *oh you will cheat on me. Oh, you will humiliate me in front of my friends.* The men have no faith in their women. Worse, the men have no faith in themselves.

But I am pleased that Dalal thought enough of her son to buy me a hijab. She is a good mother and a good friend. Along with my hijab, I am also wearing what I call my Jackie O's, the sunglasses show only my nose, lips, and chin.

"It's wonderful that you are here," I say to Aabid. "I want to see more of the Medina and I have been looking for a boy like you to protect me."

Aabid looks at his mother.

"Are you up to that?" Dalal says.

"I am not a protector."

"I know a protector when I see one," I say to the boy.

"You are mistaken, ma'am."

"I am a doctor. We don't make mistakes." There are times when a lie can serve a greater purpose.

"What sort of doctor?" the boy says. He is suspicious.

"I am an anthropologist."

"What is that? I do not know this profession."

"I study different cultures and social systems."

"You should study my deceased father's sister," Aabid says. The boy is still preoccupied with his bruised knee. He has licked the tip of his index finger and he is tracing the bruise with saliva. "Auntie Arub, this is her name. It means 'loving to her husband.' This is a name I do not understand. Auntie Arub was never married and she is not loving to anyone. This is a woman with emotional problems. I believe you are the very person to study her, Doctor. This is a woman who will yell at a young boy without the slightest provocation. Perhaps he did not wipe his shoes before coming into the home. Perhaps he forgot to do one of his chores. A boy who does not forget a chore or two is not really a boy. Don't you agree, Doctor? Auntie Arub's problems are deep and many."

"This is not respectful talk," Dalal says, whispering it. She is rubbing Aabid's back with the flat of her hand.

"I could not live with her."

"Your Auntie is a complex person."

"You are too kind," the boy says.

"It's the truth. That whole side of our family is complex." Dalal pats her son's good knee as a way to calm him. "Your father could also be very difficult," she says. "There was one way to do things for him. Anything else was not worth discussing. What are we to do? You must learn to forgive and get along."

"Poppa used to say a boy has to earn the respect of his elders." Aabid is looking back and forth, first to his mother and then to me. He says, "But if it is true for the boy, shouldn't it be true of everyone? Didn't Poppa say respect is not given for free?"

"We must respect our elders," Dalal says again. She is such a composed, even-tempered person. She says, "If our elders do not live as perfect as we would like them to, this does not matter. We respect them because they have lived longer than us. To live in this world and to live with all the horrible things that happen to us in this world, that deserves our respect."

"Even if they are crazy?"

"Especially if they are crazy, Aabid."

"This is a puzzle."

"The world is not easy for any of us."

"I have felt like you," I say to Aabid, joining in. It's my feeble try to heal whatever is wrong with whoever is in front of me. But I like this boy. There is a sweetness in him and a helplessness. "We are different but the same," I say. The helpless part in him I remember in myself when I was his age and in the camp. I tell him, "I know you are frustrated with your Auntie. It's good you are here with your mom and me. Sometimes we have to get away from what bothers us so we can see it in another light. Hopefully, a more appealing light."

"There is no such light for Auntie Arub."

"Well, you could be right."

"That's not very helpful," Dalal says to me.

AABID HAS RETRIEVED a thin roll of paper money from the inside pocket of his gray suitcoat. The boy is looking down at the dirham, weighing the roll in his open palm.

"I want to buy American cowboy boots at the market," Aabid says. I can tell he is happy to be away from his aunt and with his mother. Then he says to me, "I have saved this money from my job. I work after my lessons for a potter and he pays me good wages. I work on weekends too."

Dalal has a sudden worried look.

"I have never liked that idea," she says.

"My school grades do not suffer."

"This is what you say now."

"It is a mother's job to worry," he says to me.

"I still believe this job may interfere with your schooling," Dalal tells him. She is studying his face. "Schooling is everything, Aabid. You can buy many more items if you finish your schooling."

"I am an honor student."

"You can get married and buy a house and have children," Dalal says. She is brushing something invisible off the shoulder of his gray suitcoat. "You can know the bliss of being a father with a good job. You can see the love in the eyes of your children."

"Could we go to the Medina tomorrow?" Aabid says. He is counting his dirham slowly, one bill at a time. "I would very much like to buy the American cowboy boots with the silver toes. I have seen Eric Clapton sing on the television and wear these boots with the silver toes. He sings 'I Shot the Sheriff.' Such a very excellent song. And I have thought to myself, 'Would not Khalid envy my purchase?' Who would not respect a person with such wonderful boots?"

Dalal and Aabid continue to discuss why it is safe and not safe to go into the Medina. Their talk shifts from English to Arabic and back again.

As I listen to them I start to think about the meeting this evening with my father's longtime friend Leon Nauman. "You should not dismiss

Leon," I hear my father saying. "The old man gets the job done. But perhaps getting the job done is not something you really want. Have you thought about that, Liora? Perhaps you would prefer a more incompetent person."

I feel my stomach go tight. I am looking forward to this meeting with Leon and I am not looking forward to it. But is anyone ever ready to step into the new and unfamiliar?

TEN

I DON'T DRESS UP FOR him but I look presentable. Black linen slacks, a white silk blouse, I want to show myself as an employer, a professional person. I am not at ease in the role of an employer. I believe it's because part of me is still a thirteen-year-old who has yet to leave Theresienstadt and that hideous nightmare.

The brass clock on the mantle reads five-thirty in the evening now, maybe closer to six. Then I begin waiting for him by reading three long articles in *The Journal of Cultural Anthropology*. That's two articles more than I usually read.

No Leon Nauman.

I watch the tourists and the locals beneath my hotel window. The traffic is less noisy along the

Rue de la Liberté during Ramadan. I stay at the window until the sun has become big and orange and level with the horizon. Against an evening sky I see lamps being lighted on the minarets to signal another day of fasting is at an end.

But still no Leon.

Later I wake to knocking and a voice on the other side of the door. I have been sleeping on the couch and I do not know who is saying my name or where I am. An old panicky feeling heats my chest and stomach. This feeling is what woke me at night when I was a girl in Theresienstadt.

"…Liora?" The voice is slightly more than a whisper, a man's voice. Knock. Knock. "Liora? Open the door." Knock, knock. There are far off drums and flutes and rhythmic clapping coming through the open window. Okay yes, I do remember. It's another day of Ramadan. Hungry people are eating dates and drinking bowls of Harira and glasses of milk. Now I hear the man's voice again. He sounds old and tired and annoyed. "Hey, how about you opening the damn door, Liora?"

"…Leon?" I look at my wristwatch. It's sixteen to eleven. He was supposed to be here at six and I am ready to tell him to come back tomorrow.

"I got vodka," he says. Knock, knock. And adds, "I also got olives."

"Wait a minute."

This definitely gets me walking toward the door.

After I let Leon Nauman in and he fixes us two vodkas with olive brine and olives, I decide not to chide him for being five hours behind schedule. Vodka has a way of letting most people forgive almost anything.

"You're looking very nice," Leon says. "This is an elegant outfit. I like it."

"Don't push your luck."

"It's a compliment."

"I know what it is."

Leon is thinner and more fragile than I remember. When he was a younger man he had a bulky compressed body and dark thick hair and very dark eyes and his eyes made me want to run into my room and lock the door. He could terrorize a person with those eyes. But now he no longer presents as a serious man and that is oddly sad. Everything about him has a washed out and worn out look. Of course I have not seen him in twenty years, maybe a year or two longer than that. Our conversations over the last six months or so since my father hired him are rare and when we do talk we talk by phone. His hair is wispy and the darkness of it is gone. I can see the bones in his cheeks and the veins in his hands.

"How's Dad?" I say.

"The usual aches and pains," he tells me. "What

can I say? We're getting older. Him, me, you, nothing stays the same." Leon undoes the two straps to his leather briefcase. It was eighty-three degrees today in Tangier with a nice breeze from the ocean but Leon is wearing tan corduroy pants and a matching vest. His wrinkled shirt is flannel and rolled unevenly above skinny wrists. He is dressed for winter. "We have problems with your Colonel," he says and shuffles through the briefcase until he finds a file-sized manila envelope. "This is a guy who likes the upper hand, a guy who wants to be in charge, if you get my drift."

"Tell me the news, Leon, the good and the bad."

"The Colonel's health shits."

"That's your good news?"

"Yeah. In a manner of speaking."

"And the bad?"

"He's breathing."

"Why is that?"

"…pardon?"

"Why is the Colonel *still* breathing?"

How does that happen? Nazis were tried by the thousands. When people think about war trials they think of Nuremburg, the major war criminals. But there were more trials than that. There were the Doctors trial, the Milch and the Judges trials. They had the Pohl, Flick and the IG Farben trials. The Hostages trial, the Russian trial. Many, many. There were also trials in other countries, Austria, the Netherlands, Germany, Italy, Japan, and so on and so on. We jailed and executed Nazis all over the world. So how did Colonel K. P. Kohler get out of that?

Who did he know?

Why wasn't he hunted down?

Off and on my family and I have searched for Colonel Kohler. Leon is one of several investigators employed over the years.

"He should get sick before his due," I now tell Leon. After all my thoughts on the matter, this is my answer to his news that Colonel Kohler's health has not been good.

"The colonel has been sick for years," Leon says. Leon is balancing his briefcase on his lap with his left hand while using his right to sip the vodka. "The man was born with a bad heart," he says. "This is nothing new. Some people are born with bad luck. The man also had a couple of strokes, including a recent one. Gets himself around in a wheelchair."

"Does he live alone?"

"Uh-huh. But he has a nephew who helps."

"He should have been caught and prosecuted."

"Nazis had information to sell. Colonel Kohler is a man who knows everybody. Theresienstadt wasn't a killing center. You know that better than me, Liora. It had two purposes, to let the old and infirm die and to transport the healthy ones to the killing centers in the east.

"So, he made a deal."

"With Allied Intelligence, yes.

"He testified?"

"At Nuremburg. And at some of the camp trials, too. Auschwitz. Belsen. He was responsible for shipping prisoners. You get to know who's in charge of what. You get information you can use after the war. Colonel Kohler is a bastard but he's a bastard who thinks ahead."

"And he got our protection."

"Very good, Doc."

"I'm sure the Israelis love that."

"The Israelis have learned patience."

"This is home? Tangier?"

"Now, yes. But the man has lived everywhere. Different names, different passports. The name he uses here is Hartmut Becker."

Lamps on the end tables bring light and shadows to the white walls of the hotel room. The windows are open and the night is cool. I still hear the music coming from the Grand Socco. It's past eleven and the talk and the laughter has not diminished. There is the smell of the ocean and the pine trees. The people here are very reverent and when the fasting is done they are very hungry and fill themselves with food.

"""BUT YOU ARE not telling me the current problem,"
I say. "It doesn't feel like you have done what we
paid you to do. 'The man who likes the upper hand,'
what does that mean, Leon? 'The man who wants
to be in charge.' Tell me why I am having trouble
understanding this. And tell me, please, that I have
not traveled here for nothing, I want to hear that
most of all."

"There is a network in Tangier," he says. "Three
others, officers who worked with Kohler. Alker,
Dasch, and Johan Bering, these are the men who
worked with him at Theresienstadt. In addition,
we have civilians who are paid to listen and bring
the others information. It's a network, Liora, a very
good network, very efficient. If you run long enough
you learn *how* to run, what to do."

"I thought these people had protection?"

"To a point. But why would Kohler trust the
CIA? He knows they are using him. And one day
they'll be done with him. Besides, why would anyone trust the CIA? I wouldn't, would you?"

"Then what do you *have* for me?"

"He will contact you," Leon says.

"He will what?"

"He will contact you, that's the word."

"Well how lovely for me."

"He's going to see you, Liora."

"And how long will that be? How long do I stay in Tangier? A month, a year? I want to see him but not at the expense of my job, my work. I think you're right. This is machismo crap. This is who's in charge of whom. It's Theresienstadt all over again. It's Colonel Smiley strutting up and down his office with his little black cigar and his shiny boots."

"But you're here now. Will you leave?"

"You said he was living alone?"

"Yes, but he's being cared for by a relative, a nephew." Leon places the leather briefcase by the edge of his chair and crosses his legs. His socks are black and gather about his ankles and reveal the start of thin hairless legs. "It's his brother's son."

"I didn't know he had a brother."

"Fairly wealthy," Leon says. He uses a forefinger and thumb to pull at one of his socks but the sock will not stay up. "The man owns art galleries in Berlin and Hamburg. Or did, maybe still does. Both brothers were educated in England, the Colonel at Cambridge and Christophe at Chelsea College of Art and Design. Apparently, Christophe was the talented one."

"This brother, he didn't join up?"

"He processed most of the stolen art. The Nazis loved art."

"They loved many things."

I DO NOT think of Colonel K. P. Kohler as having a family. I think of him as this slender and meticulous man, his uniform always starched, fresh, not a hint of sweat anywhere. His manicured nails, his rimless glasses, a black cigar tucked at the corner of his mouth, the man probably remained tidy throughout the war. And now that I think about it, his English did sound British. Funny how we forget. He was impeccable and courteous and had an even temperament and a smile that disregarded circumstance.

"Let her continue with him," Mother had said to Father. She was discussing the time I spent with the Colonel.

"This is our Liora. How can you say that?"

"We are fighting for our lives, Jakub."

"But it's our daughter."

"It's our lives. And Liora's life."

"No, no. Too much, Elzbieta."

That was dinner conversation, one night after the other. We were living in our little white house then, with its shutters and its glass in the windows. The sort of house my mother used to dream about in Prague. Now she had her house but it was in the middle of Theresienstadt. Our dining room table had a fancy white cloth and on top of that cloth was a silver serving dish with either a roasted chicken or maybe lamb chops or a brisket, depending on the day, and the other silver dishes held a revolving medley of peas and carrots and various types of potatoes.

As we ate, I could hear the talk and the praying in the barracks that circled our house. I heard other prisoners calling out to us, to me. Some of them called for help, to use our influence. This is also when I heard them calling us names. I have talked about that before. The name calling never varied. My mother and I were always the Nazi bitches or the Nazi whores. They said our cunts smelled from Nazi dick. *Tvoje matka je kunda smrdi jako nacisticky curak!* they'd yell. My father was Hitler's physician or Goering's physician or Sauckel's physician or Hoss's physician, any big deal Nazi they could think of. They forgot the times my father had helped them. How he had argued with Colonel Kohler and the others for medications. Prisoners would call out to me, too. They told me to run. They told me to stop being the colonel's whore child. *Nistaly nacisticke devka!* they'd yell.

"...HE LIVES IN the Medina," Leon Nauman is saying.

I'm sitting across from Leon on the sofa and looking at the vodka and olive in my glass. The night air comes through the open window and the air is cool and clean. I am feeling the effects of the vodka, too. That light in the shoulders feeling, how I love that. The world could be collapsing around me and I would look here and there and see it as an amusing distraction.

"You listening, Liora?"

"That was sweet to remember the vodka."

"Your Colonel lives in the Medina."

"I heard you, Leon. I'm not deaf."

"You're something." Leon shakes his head at what he sees as my lack of interest.

"What sort of something?"

"It's an expression," he says and appears bewildered at my response. "For years, you have obsessed about this Colonel," he says. "Now that you have the information, you don't seem that interested."

"I want to find him. I do not want him to 'find me.' There's something insulting in that. I am far too old to be thirteen again."

"Who cares who does what?"

"I do, *I* care."

I am looking at the lights outside my hotel window, the moon and the many stars in the night sky. I see ships in the North Atlantic. Red and yellow lights are specks on a black horizon.

"Did you tell me there was a nephew?"

"He visits," Leon says. "Takes him out, pushes the wheelchair. That sort of thing. They seem to prefer an after-dinner stroll."

"Do you have a name?"

"…the nephew? Willem, I think."

"Oh really?"

"I believe so, yes."

I cannot hide the excitement I feel.

I am thinking, Willem as in Eloise and Willem. I'm thinking, the Willem who beats the hell out of his lovely wife – *that* Willem. And, yes, the lovely wife did tell me her husband was taking care of an uncle.

Well Eloise, dear…we must have a talk.

Eleven

THREE DAYS BEFORE MY TRIP to Tangier, I drove to my parents' house in Norfolk. I was upstairs in the attic looking through things, my mother behind me, her arms crossed and watching my every move. The woman is very thin and wears her hair in a French bun and she had on her pearls and her white blouse with the high collar.

"What are you looking for, Liora?"

"I'll find it."

"But I could help."

"You're getting me nervous."

"How can I get you nervous? I'm your mother."

"Yes, I know. Pretend I'm not here."

Morning sunlight was coming through the tiny window at the peak of the roof and the light was yellow, dusty and bright on the wood planks of the floor and it went through the narrow attic and cut the shadows in the corners.

"If you would just tell me," Mother said.

"You're making it difficult to think."

"Well it's not on purpose. You're my child. I want to help, it's my nature."

"Where's the dress?"

"…I'm sorry. What?"

"The dress. And the shoes, the patent leather shoes. I know you have them. And *please* do not tell me you don't have them or you can't remember where you've put them because I know that's bullshit."

"Ladies don't use those words."

"The dress and shoes, please."

"What are you talking about?"

The attic smelled of cedar and damp wool.

"Is that it?" I pointed to a polished wood trunk in a corner and half concealed by shadow. It had the look of a big pirate's chest.

"Your father and I don't see you for months, Liora. No visits, no letters, no calls, nothing. *Nothing*. I mean it's as if we don't exist, that we've disappeared from the face of the earth. Your father and I are the people who brought you into this world – into *this* world, thank you." Her hands fluttered and twitched with her words. "Then suddenly you're in my attic, acting like a crazy person."

"I'm not a crazy person."

"You know what I mean," Mother said. "It's an expression." As I opened the pirate's trunk she says, "No, no. You can't just come into my house, your *father's* house, and go through our things. These are private things."

"It's in the trunk, isn't it?"

"You need to wait for your father."

"Hey. I used to live here, too."

The inside of the pirate's trunk smelled of cedar and mothballs. There were folded sweaters in see-through plastic bags. There were folded towels and blankets. And beneath these things, wrapped in air-tight plastic and laced with moth balls, I discovered a young girl's lavender and crinoline dress, her black patent leather shoes. *My* dress. *My* patent leather shoes. Thirty years had passed and the silk and crinoline had a finely thready look but the shoes were fine.

I lifted the plastic bag from the trunk and examined the dress and shoes in the dusty light coming through the attic window.

"Put that back," my mother said. "Do you hear what I am saying, Liora?" Her slender hands had become more animated, more frantic with her words. "That's part of our family's history, it's part of a historic time. What is wrong with you? What world are you living in? That's not yours to take.

Are you listening to me? Put it back, put it back now."

"It's my dress, my shoes. These things were gifts. What right do you have to take my gifts, to hide these things?"

"You never showed an interest."

"What was I supposed to do, Mother? Press the stuff in a book like a wrist corsage from the senior prom? This has nothing to do with what's wrong with *me*. I'm the one who had to deal with the Colonel. Thirteen years old and *I* was dealing with him. Not you. *Me*."

"Is that what you believe? Do you really think this is *all* just about you? My God, we were trying to survive. Have you forgotten that? We were in Theresienstadt. And this Colonel Kohler, this awful, gruesome man, gave us a house, the most wonderful house we'd ever known. You don't remember our life before the camp? Has it been so long that you have lost what is real and what isn't? We lived in one room above your father's office. We had no money, his patients were the poorest of the poor. They bartered with him, these patients. Butter and bread, poultry and fish, you don't get rich on fish and bread."

"I'm taking what belongs to me."

"But why now, Liora? I don't understand."

I didn't completely understand, either. I was

going to Tangier, a chance to give some peace to that thirteen-year-old girl in me, a chance to see and talk to the Colonel again. The dress and the shoes seemed part of all that.

It was Miss Reba's idea, really. She once said, "The things we gather from our past have an energy, a life. These things can lead us back to those times." I believe the dress and the shoes will help me think about what I need to do.

I REMEMBER THIS argument from the old days. We were in the little white house in the center of Theresienstadt. We wanted a peaceful island amid an on-going nightmare. Or at least the illusion of peace. My parents would feel blessed one minute and traitors the next. None of us found peace. The good food, the comfortable beds, we were happy to have them. Yet there were many nights where we couldn't eat or sleep.

Even in my parents most positive, hopeful moments, the conversations became extraordinary.

"Look at the food," Mother had said.

"We have real beds," my father said. "Do you want to go back to sleeping on wooden bunks and living in a barracks with windows that have no glass to keep out the cold? Is that what you want, Liora?"

"They pray all night," Mother said.

"You want to go back to that?" Father wanted to know. "The crying and the praying? What sort of life is that?"

"This place doesn't belong to us," I said.

"Homes don't belong to the people who live in them," Father said. "People have mortgages." He looked at Mother. "Am I right?"

"Your father's right, dear."

"Banks, Nazis," my father said. "What's the difference?"

"I couldn't agree more, Liora."

"It's not our home." I was emphatic about this. "It's not even a home," I said. "It's for the newspapers, Daddy. It's for the journalists who come here and want to show the Nazis as evil. And the Nazis tell them, 'But wait. Look at our camp doctor. He keeps our prisoners healthy. He protects them against disease. See how we take care of the doctor and his family so nothing happens to him? We care about our prisoners,' the Nazis would say. But it wasn't real. It was never real. It was their *movie*. Don't you know the Nazis used us? The Colonel put me in dresses and gave me new shoes but these things belonged to girls he'd killed or had killed. Don't you get it?"

They got it, of course. They just didn't want to hear it.

❖❖❖

MOTHER SNATCHED AT the plastic wrap that protected the lavender dress and shoes but I kept it out of her reach.

"The Colonel bought these things in Paris," she said. "He bought them especially for you, Liora. You've never accepted that fact but that's how much he thought of you, how you affected him."

"I was thirteen, a child. I had skinny legs and arms the size of twigs. I could barely stand to look at myself."

"You were a beauty. Slim, dark eyes, nice bone structure. I may not know much but I know what men find attractive."

"That's mother talk."

"You don't think I can be objective?"

"We were frightened. You and Daddy needed me."

"It was a war, Liora, everything's different in war. Values change, they shift, people have to survive. You were a lovely girl then and you're still lovely. And that's not just a mother talking. I *know* lovely. Yes, we were trying to get through difficult times. How can anyone in their right mind deny the times were not difficult? But there are girls who'd run to the bathroom and throw up to be thin like you. Like you were, like you are *now*. You're a beauty now."

I know my mother loves me. And believe it, I do love her, both my parents. But there are times she and Daddy are too much, fussing over me, compliments and such. It gets me uncomfortable. Then there are times they go into some other universe.

"It's true," she says.

"Colonel Kohler pulled the dress and the shoes from a pile of clothes left by the children. Don't you remember all the clothing, a pile from the men, from the women, the boys and the girls? You don't remember? They emptied their suitcases before taking the trains to the east."

"I remember the piles of clothing, Liora. I'm not stupid. I'm just saying you were a beauty, you still are. You're blessed. What's wrong with that? Maybe you're right. But I will always believe that particular dress and shoes came from Paris. What I *do* remember is the look on his face when he watched you. I know love when I see it."

I SUPPOSE I'D thought that, too. Colonel K.P. Kohler had been in love with me. And if I'm honest with myself, I would have to say I liked knowing he loved me and I also believed I loved him back. I loved him the way a frightened girl loves the beast that has her life in its hands. In my adolescent narcissism, I imagined the Colonel and I as *Beauty and the Beast. Belle et Bête.* I loved him the way a young girl loves a fierce and volatile protector.

What can I say? The heart does what it is going to do. The heart humbles the influential and uplifts the weak.

Isn't that how love works?

Love is mysterious because it is not a conscious decision. It is not "I'll take two of these and three of those." Anyone who weighs the pros and cons of a suitor's love is calculating an investment.

"…THEY WERE ALL crazy," Mother was saying. She'd been talking about the people in Theresienstadt, the soldiers, the prisoners, everybody. "…the war and what we did in the war or we had to do – it has to get a person crazy."

The plastic wrap with the dress and shoes lay across my arm. Dusty yellow light from the attic window glinted off the plastic and the patent leather shoes. Mother and I had started on our way down the stairs.

"I think that sometimes. Even at thirteen, a part of me knew Colonel Kohler was crazy," I said. "I knew he was a very unhappy man and I knew he didn't have a conscience. That's a volatile combination, a depressed man with no restraint. If you have a conscience and you're unhappy enough, maybe you'll just kill yourself. Never a good thing but at least nobody dies but you. That's very different from an individual who has *no* conscience. An unhappy person with no conscience needs to have a lot of room."

"I'm sure the Colonel was quite sane."

"You didn't know him."

"Well not like you, of course. But Colonel Kohler was very polite to me. And to your father. He was very courteous to us, always a smile."

"Didn't that strike you as odd?"

"Being friendly? No."

"I don't know how you've survived, Mother. Truly, I don't. I think about that occasionally and get the shivers. It's like a drunk who never dies from a fall. I cannot imagine what amount of luck it took for you to get from there to here."

I HAD WATCHED Colonel Kohler shoot prisoners from his office window for personal amusement. This terrified and excited me. And yet. And yet. Though I do not remember my exact thinking, I must have felt safe with him. Or as safe as a teenager can feel in a world that was more vicious and unpredictable than Colonel Kohler. The Colonel was no more than a subdued reflection of that world. Being loved by him gave my family a pass. He allowed us to live in a freshly painted white house with windows and shutters. The Colonel fed us good food and gave us thick blankets for our beds. He gave me dresses and pretty shoes. He had dinner with me in his office.

I was too naïve to know the control I wielded over him. What I had was the power of innocence. I had my youth and my sexuality. But I did not know about such things, that power. By the time I did know, the time of that power had come and gone.

Once after dinner in his office the Colonel gave me his sidearm and lifted my hand and the pistol in it to his head and commanded me to pull the trigger. He knew I could not do it. He'd been drinking wine and was being amusing, or his idea of amusing. His humor was too dark for a girl of thirteen.

It's too dark for a woman of forty-two.

"What's wrong, darling?"

"I can't do this," I'd told him.

"You squeeze the trigger."

"I know what to do," I said. "I don't want to do it."

"See this is your problem," the Colonel said. He had actually cocked the pistol for me. "You are too young and your heart is too sweet," he said. "You will always be at a loss if you do not at least have this choice in your repertoire. Tell me please," the Colonel said. "How will you get through this world with a heart like that?"

TWELVE

I HAVE DONE THE BEST I can do with her. I cleaned the blood about her nose and upper lip. There is also a small cut on the right side of her face near the eye that I examined. Nothing here looks that bad but nothing looks that good, either. The area beneath the eye and the cut itself are very swollen and bruised and may already be infected.

"My God," I said as I was cleaning her. "What happened to you?" But I knew the answer. You know it exactly, Liora, I'm thinking. Why I do I ask a question when the answer is staring me in the face?

Eloise will not discuss it.

She knocked on the door less than ten minutes ago. We are now sitting on the sofa in my hotel room. It has decided to rain this morning and the sky is gray and the breeze coming through the windows smells of wet pine. I gave her a cold damp washcloth to press against her cut to stop the swelling.

"You need to go to a hospital," I tell her.

"It looks worse than it is."

"You might need a suture." I move her hand that holds the washcloth and examine the redness, the bruise and the swelling for a second time. I am thinking it's all right but nobody should get cavalier with this sort of thing. Then I say, "I'd get myself an x-ray for a possible fracture. You ought not to pretend everything is fine."

"I'm not sure why I came." She won't look at me.

"I think you are very sure."

"Then you know more than I do."

"About some things."

I WANTED TO ask about Willem and the Colonel. I wanted to do that when Eloise first walked into my room. Was Leon right? Is Willem the nephew? But she looked in too much pain and my questions felt far too opportunistic. I am ashamed to even think it. How often does Willem visit his uncle? Do they get along? What sort of relationship do they have with each other? Could you possibly tell me where the uncle lives? It's okay, really. I am a friend from years and years ago, we knew each other very well, the Colonel and me.

I cannot do it.

But I'm *going* to do it, I think to myself. I *have* to do it. The entire time we were in Theresienstadt I waited on the Colonel's beck and call. Those times are gone, many years gone, and I am not waiting around for him to beckon me again.

We change, all of us. And I want him to know that. More really, *I* want to know it myself, I want to feel it. I want to know the difference between thirteen and forty-two. There is a difference, isn't there? Or is this a question like the agelessness of the eternal spirit? Are we nothing but children in old bodies?

"I DON'T WANT to discuss how awful this or that person is," Eloise is saying. The washcloth is pressed to her face and she is looking down at her lap. She has on a green and white flowered terry cloth robe and slippers. Her thick blond hair drapes and hides her face. The hair is tangled and does not look as if it has been combed this morning. "I am not that sort of person," she says. "I am not one of those women."

"What sort of women are we talking about?"

"The complainers. I hate them."

"I don't see you as a complainer."

"You know what I mean."

"This doesn't get better," I say. "People do not snap their fingers and change their personalities, and that includes your husband. If we could do that, psychotherapists would be out of a job. Who would need them?"

Eloise has walked over to the open window. Her hands are on the white sill and her face is leaning toward the breeze from the Atlantic. It's raining and the air is chilled and the breeze has already dampened her face. The smell of the ocean and the umbrella pines drift through the windows. Her hair flutters about her eyes and forehead.

"This is not our usual situation," she tells me. Her voice is quiet as if she does not want to talk but feels obligated by my presence. Her quiet voice is the compromise. "It's not an easy trip for him. Willem loves Berlin; he loves his routine. You know how men are. God forbid you should upset their routines. But he says things will be different soon."

"It takes work to change," I say and watch her from the sofa. Eloise's back is to me and she tightens the flowered robe and folds her arms in front of her. I am not sure how far I should go with this. I do not want to stir up feelings that would drive her away but I do not want Willem to hurt her again. I tell her, "If you think everything is going to be okay or things will be different, or if you believe Willem will be a different man tomorrow, then you do not know how this works."

"Men get angry when they feel helpless."

"Some do." I decide to step back. I won't get anywhere brow-beating her. I say, "Aren't you getting cold standing by that window?"

"There are reasons people act the way they do," she says.

"No argument, believe me."

"Willem isn't an evil man," Eloise says. She has turned and walks from the window to the sofa and sits beside me, tucking a leg under her. "I am aware you didn't say he was evil but I want you to know that it's true," she says. "I want you to know he is not evil. He can be a very loving. Most of time he is very loving. I won't go on with this if you insist on making my husband out to be a villain."

"Villains are for the movies, dear."

"People are more complex."

"I agree."

"He's feeling very helpless now." Eloise is patting the dampness from her face with the sleeve of her robe. "What with his family and all, his elderly uncle," she says. "We came here for Willem's family."

"I remember you mentioned that."

Yes, that's a good place to start, the uncle. This is what I am thinking. Was the uncle an influence on Willem's behavior? Have you ever met Willem's uncle? If so, did you find him a charming or an evil man? There is much confusion in my family over this point. Charming or evil, that is the family argument, the left and the right of it, as if one must choose one or the other, as if the notion of a charmingly evil man does not exist. I don't think it's an "either or," I have never thought that.

"Men hate feeling helpless."

"Don't we all."

"But men in particular," Eloise says. "I mean don't you think? Men have to do something, solve something." As she dries her face with the sleeve of her robe her arm becomes exposed. Her arm is thin and pale and blue veins show through the skin. "Most men are so what-you-call-it, goal oriented. That's what people say. If they can't solve a problem, they go nuts. Am I right? You study cultures, different people. You're a..." She does not know what to call me.

"Anthropologist."

"Anthropologist. Don't men go nuts?"

"THIS IS THE uncle you said had the stroke?"

That is the question I finally ask her, my way in, the way that can lead her to other questions. I do not feel good about it but I have traveled to Tangier to meet with Colonel Kohler and I should keep that in the forefront of my mind. I like Eloise and I'd like to help her but there must be a *quid pro quo*, whether known or not.

"Yes, a stroke," Eloise says in a dismissive way. "An elderly man but a pain, you know? Oh, I tell my husband, 'Look, Willem, you expect too much of yourself. You are not God. You can't make old people young. You don't have that power.' I mean a wife should support her husband, right? Be objective and all. I tell him, 'You are too hard on yourself. People get old. Everybody gets old, okay?' But he does not pay attention to me. Willem is a good man but he is a stubborn man."

"So, Willem loves his uncle."

"Yes, but it's the money, too. That's what Willem says. His uncle has money from the war. Also, there's art and jewelry; gold, mostly. Willem says you can love someone very much and still hope they will put you in their will. He likes to joke about that."

"I didn't know there was a will?"

"Oh yes. We think his uncle has a lot of money. And believe me, we need money. Willem is a designer. Men's clothes? You should see some of his sketches. He's a very talented person. We want to open a shop in Paris, maybe Milan. But it's expensive to start such a business.

"Why not have your business in Germany?"

"There's no such thing as German fashion."

"I suppose you're right," I say. "I don't hear about German fashion."

"That's what Willem says."

"The uncle is very sick?"

"Well I don't know about *very* sick," she says. "That's a strong word and all. But he had the stroke. Also heart problems, heart operations."

"How old is he?"

"Old. In his sixties, sixty-something."

Ah, an old man. I try not to smile. When I was Eloise's age I used to think life was over at sixty but the closer I get to sixty the younger it looks and the more grateful I am to the people who celebrate that age. Sixty is old to people who are thirty and younger but it is a blessing to us who are forty and older. When I see a sixty-year-old finish, say, a triathlon, I cheer and applaud and think to myself, well if that man or that woman can do such a thing, why shouldn't I be able to live a longer, healthier life."

Don't we all think this?

Don't we cheer for the possibility of a few extra years? It's true, isn't it? I want to see a sixty-year-old out there huffing and puffing. That sixty-year-old does not have to cross the finish line first to get my applause, either. Just make it to the end, crawl over the finish line. Breathe heavy, grasp your chest, I do not care. But finish the damn race. Give us forty-somethings a reason to cheer.

"How many operations?" I am talking about the uncle now.

"Three or four," Eloise says. She has hidden her hands in the opposite sleeves of her robe like the Japanese do with a kimono. "The man had his first surgery when he was a boy, ten or eleven. I think that's what Willem said."

"So perhaps genetic. Anything else?"

"Recently, he had pneumonia."

"And almost died, I bet."

"Very close. That's why we're here, Willem and me." Eloise goes over to the window and shuts it. She does a little shiver and says, "It's getting cold. You don't mind?"

"That's fine, dear."

"I don't want to seem like I own the place."

"You're not doing anything of the sort."

Eloise gives me a little smile that is here and gone. Then she lowers her head and all that hair hides whatever expression comes next. It's sweet and sad; I like her very much. She plays peek-a-boo with people.

I suspect I know who tells her to stop acting like she owns the place but I am an anthropologist and not a therapist and I don't need to help her get insight. I do know that this type of male-female behavior happens in most cultures. And I am no different than the people I study. Many times, I have lied to myself about who I am and about who the people are who are closest to me. I also know that if I am honest I cannot step away from being the observer, being the witness. This is more than what I do. It's who I am and it has made for shitty relationships and conversations. Or at least very uncomfortable ones. But I am also worried about Eloise and I do not trust the husband.

"Did Willem hit you before his uncle got sick?" I say.

"I don't want to talk about that, anymore."

"He did, yes?"

"My husband is not open for discussion."

That's not all together true. Eloise is still here. Hoping for something, I believe. What we have to do is figure out a way to talk about the things we want to talk about without scaring each other to death.

❖ ❖ ❖

I PAT THE spot on the sofa beside me for Eloise to come and sit. When she is settled next to me, I say, "Most of us think we know how people work but we don't have a clue. It's absolutely true. The work I do is not easy. It's not easy for people of other cultures to talk about themselves with me and it's not easy for me to grasp everything they tell me. These people aren't complainers. They are very much like us. They protect the husbands who hit them, fiercely protect them. What you have basically are men who hit women. And after they hit them the men tell the women why they love them too much. As if this love is the perfect reason for hitting them. It's true for most cultures. Does that sound familiar?"

"Willem does love me."

"There are better versions of love."

"You do not see him cry."

"I've seen men cry," I say and place two fingers under her chin and lift her head up and the curtain of hair slips away to show her face. "The men who hit the women they love become remorseful but they hit them again. That's what they do. That's what they'll always do. And in too many cultures to name. Some of these men were hit as children. It's what they were taught. Is that the life you want?

And if you do want that life, then what is wrong with you?"

"Willem is not like that all the time."

"So, he only beats you on Tuesdays?"

"That's not fair."

"None of it is fair, dear."

"You don't listen very well," Eloise says. She is upset but she is upset with the possibility of getting at the truth of this thing. And she says, "My husband is feeling helpless now. He doesn't want to lose this man who's been practically a father to him. Okay? Weren't you paying attention? Didn't you hear me? There are things you don't know. You can't make a judgment when you don't know the facts."

"What fact says he should beat you?"

"I'm going. This was a mistake."

"No, this was very smart and very brave."

"I love Willem."

"I know you do," I tell her. I rest the palm of my hand on her shoulder. Her body is quivering. "And I am not saying he doesn't love you. What I am saying is, this sort of love can be very dangerous."

I am talking about Eloise's marriage but I can't quit thinking about Willem and the uncle. This is how I am. I get something in my mind and the thing attaches itself to my consciousness like one of those little sucker fish that ride on the bellies of sharks.

I have always been that way. Daddy used to call it my radar. He'd tell people, "Don't ever let Liora get you on her radar."

"The uncle," I say, "This is Willem's father's brother?"

"…yes." Eloise has a cautious tone.

"What is your last name?"

"You mean my married name?"

"Yes, your married name."

"Kohler."

It's amazing to hear the Colonel's name coming from Eloise. When she speaks his name the bridges of time and casualness dissolve between us. I can actually feel my neck and cheeks heating up as parts of the world click into place. Willem is in Tangier waiting for his uncle to die, waiting for the money. Leon is right. It always annoys me when the man is right; I don't know why. Then my thoughts go to the Colonel. I think, your money is just another little white house, isn't it? You love keeping us close to you with hints of paradise.

I decide to take my chance. I don't want to lie to her and I don't want to frighten her. Honesty is always preferable to anything else.

"I am here in Tangier to see Willem's uncle," I

say. "K.P. Kohler helped me when I was a girl. He helped my family and I get through a very bad time during the war. I have often thought of seeing him again and thanking him."

I am not being completely honest but I am being honest enough.

Eloise looks at me and does not say anything, not at first. I can see she has her suspicions. Her face loses its expression, all hints.

"How did you know Willem's uncle was here?"

"I hired an investigator, a friend of my father's," I say. "He's really professional. But Willem's uncle has been traveling for a long time. He knows how to do it, I will give that to the man. How to get from there to here. My investigator says Colonel Kohler is going to contact me very soon but I worry about the time. I'm a professor, I have a job, responsibilities, a limited amount of money. I've no way to reach the Colonel, to tell him of my dilemma. Then I heard you talking about your husband caring for a sick uncle and what you said about the uncle's money, the 'war' money."

"Willem said that." Eloise had a tremble to her voice. "I was only saying what Willem said, that's all. I don't know anything about the uncle or what goes on between them."

"I understand, believe me." I gave Eloise what I hoped was an empathic smile. "Best to keep out of such things. Who knows what goes on between relatives, yes? But I was thinking, you know? This would certainly show Willem in a positive light, his true devotion, so-to-speak, a nephew worthy of being remembered."

"You mean his uncle's will."

"Well putting two good friends in touch with one another, what could be better? I'm sure the Colonel would be pleased and I would certainly put in a good word about such thoughtfulness."

"Willem has been so fussy lately."

"Yes, we'll have to fix that, won't we?"

"I worry about Willem."

"Oh, I know you do."

Thirteen

I WAKE AT 3:34 AM and I am scared and I don't know why. My white cotton t-shirt is wet beneath my arms and across my shoulders. I want to say this feeling is without a context but that is not true. This talk about meeting with Colonel Kohler is stirring things up. Close to thirty years have passed and I am still in 1945. It's the year that does not end. There are guards who will kill me to stop a boring afternoon. There are prisoners who will kill Mother and Father and me because we eat better than they do.

I sit down in the wood straight back chair next to the window and I look out at the night and the stars and St. Andrew's church on the *Rue d'Angleterre*. There are yellow street lamps and a car or two. The smell and the sound of the ocean comes through the window, the damp breeze forever present.

I RECALL MISS Reba bringing the anxieties of Theresienstadt to my attention in a different way.

In the Spring of 1959 I was preparing to leave not just Pisac but the person who had become my dearest friend in all the world, the ayahuasca shaman herself, Miss Reba. I had not been able to stay an observer with her. Believe me, no one will ever judge me as severely as I'd judged myself. But in my defense, I did remain an observer to all but her. So much for objectivity, for scientific detachment. I imagined the chairman of my doctoral committee questioning my involvement with the "locals" and the validity of a year's worth of work. In the end, he did not ask and I did not confess. It was hard to leave Peru and the Sacred Valley. It was heartbreaking to leave Reba.

My year of field work had given me two medium-sized suitcases filled with hand written notes, a mix of photographs, yellow legal pads and loose paper rolled up and held together with red rubber bands. I had more data than I needed, really, enough to write two dissertations.

$$\text{❖ ❖ ❖}$$

THREE OR FOUR weeks before my departure, Miss Reba and I were walking through the Sunday market. She was wearing the black cotton pollera and a bright orange waist length vest, her gray hair braided. She also had on her father's Quechuan hat, a fedora with a good-looking feather.

The vendors had laid out their blankets on the tan stones of the square and arranged whatever they were selling on the blankets. The Spring was new and the wind was still cold and it came down from the mountains and blew the dust about the stones and quivered the big opened burlap bags of spices, the white tissue that wrapped the mangos, pears, grapes and oranges. There were hand woven fabrics and clothing. The vendors also sold jewelry, lots of opals and onyx. I saw flowers, too, lilies and orchids.

Miss Reba and I had been talking about the medicines that are in the jungle.

"My sister was a *curandera* like me" she said.

"*Curandera*," I said, mimicking her – koo-rahn-dehr-ah.

"A woman who cures with plants," Miss Reba said as she feels a turquoise fabric from one of the vendors with her thumb and forefinger. Her skin was tanned and wrinkled from age and the wind and the sun. "Our mothers and daughters do this," she said. "Men do it, too. But more the women, I think. Here it is mostly the women. I do not know about other places. I am not like you, I do not study who does what. My sister taught me how to make the ayahuasca."

"What you smoke?"

"Yes, it is milder than the drink. What I smoke is the dried vine. This is called *caapi*." Miss Reba had a leather pouch of the crushed dried vine. She took the pouch from her vest and opened it and I bent down to smell the crushed *caapi*. It was a grassy odor. Miss Reba said, "What I smoke is much like ayahuasca. But the real ayahuasca also has leaves in it and must be boiled for many hours."

I knew something about how the leaves and the vines were brewed and the rituals done with the brew but I liked it when Miss Reba talked to me and I knew I would miss our talks. When I listened to her it was like the relief of listening to a good mother reading a bedtime story I had already memorized.

"I like hearing about the rituals," I said.

"I have already talked to you about this, the rituals and so on. Haven't we talked about the rituals?" Miss Reba catches me right off.

"That's all right. I enjoy listening."

"Time for you to talk.

"Me? I'm the student."

"Good. Tell me what I have taught you."

I immediately went into my recitation mode.
"The curandera will sanctify the ayahuasca with a
sacred tobacco called the *mapacho*," I'd said this
in a casual way but I was in a big-time panic and
I hoped I would not forget some little something
of the ritual and disappoint Miss Reba. "Then the
patient and the shaman drink the ayahuasca," I
said. "The patient is usually under a blanket in a
dark hut. And the shaman will sing or chant to the
patient."

"Why does the curandera sing?"

"To enter the gateway," I said.

"Yes. And what else?"

"So, the patient will not feel alone."

"This is most important."

I also knew what Miss Reba did not know but I
had decided to keep that to myself. If she had asked
me I could have told her these things in the language of western medicine. I could have said how
the *caapi* vine has a MAO inhibitor that does not let
the drug Dimethyltryptamine or DMT metabolize
in the stomach or in the small intestine. The MAO
delivers the drug to the brain's receptors. And one
thing more, scientists now tell us the hallucinogenic
DMT is also released at our deaths with or without
the use of ayahuasca. Like a good graduate student,
I had done my research.

❖ ❖ ❖

THE WIND WAS very strong this day and everything around me fluttered and snapped, the vendors' blankets, the handmade clothes and the fabrics, the hem of Miss Reba's pollera. Sand swirled up from the stone and dirt street and batted at our faces and necks. Sand glittered in the sunlight. There were also the sounds of animals in the market, pigs and chickens. I could also smell meats and vegetables cooking on wood fires. Wonderful odors had trapped themselves in the smoke and swirled along with the wind. Mostly the Europeans and the Americans bought the pork. The locals bought the vegetables and the chickens.

"You look nervous," Miss Reba said.

"I am nervous."

"You and I have talked about this."

"Me being nervous?" I know of no such conversation.

"Every time we have gone into the market."

"…every time?"

"This should not be a surprise."

"You're thinking of another person."

"I do not confuse people."

"Well I am sad I am leaving," I said. "Maybe it's that."

I was watching the pigs and the chickens. The pigs were locked inside a small dark wood pen in the center of the market and they had no room to move. The chickens stayed pressed between the pigs. Sometimes the pigs got annoyed with the chickens and kicked them. The chickens would squawk and try to flap their wings. Feathers would go everywhere.

"I am sad you are leaving, too," Miss Reba told me.

"Maybe being sad is getting me nervous."

"That's not it."

"Then I don't know."

"It's the market," Miss Reba said.

"You've lost me." Nothing was coming to mind.

"We've talked about this."

"If you say so, I'm sure it's true."

"I have seen what the market does to you."

Why should I keep my conversations with people a secret from myself? That's what I had thought. I was not some crazy person. Isn't that what crazy people do? I did not remember any talk about the market making me nervous. Vendors brought their goods to Pisac every Sunday and the people came here from Cuzco and many other cities. This was a favorite market of the tourists and the locals who sold to the tourists. Some from the town cooked stews on open fires, Seco de Cabrito, made with goat or lamb and marinated in the local beer; Seco de Chavelo, a mix of beef and bananas.

Why would that be disturbing?

"This is a problem you and I have with our conversations," Miss Reba said. She stood in front of me to block the wind and lighted her pipe. "You remember then you do not remember."

"That's difficult to believe."

"Do you think I would lie?"

"No, no," I said. "I can't imagine you being that sort of person."

"Things can hurt us too badly," Miss Reba said.

"Is that what you think?"

"You are not the only one who does these things."

"Maybe we should all have a convention," I said. The dark wood pen had my attention again, the pigs pressed against one another, the chickens dodging the hooves of the pigs. And I said, "Me and the other crazies. We could get together and fill in blanks of our lives."

"I have upset you."

"Not on purpose, I'm sure."

"There is no good way to say these things," Miss Reba said.

"I need to stop being an emotional mess."

"You and the rest of us."

❖ ❖ ❖

As THE DAY went on, the sun was becoming more brilliant and hot and the wind still had a chill to it. Pisac is a mountain town. The heat and the cold live together but do not mingle. This was life at eleven thousand feet.

Miss Reba and I wandered about the market and looked at things together but did not talk. There were many tourists. Most of the tourists wore either jeans or shorts, some had backpacks and cameras. I did not see anyone without a hat, baseball caps, canvas hats with strangely shaped brims. Lots of sunglasses, too, particularly the wrap-around type used by mountain climbers.

I remember Miss Reba gripping both my arms and turning me toward the dark wood pen with the pigs and the chickens. The ayahuasca smoke from her pipe drifted about my eyes and my nose, the smell of burning leaves.

"Look at this," she said.

"...look where?"

"...at them."

"What do you mean? The animals?"

"Watch the pigs and the man."

A Peruvian man was in front of the wood pen. He had on a thick orange and yellow poncho and a brown felt fedora like Miss Reba's, what is called the Quechuan hat.

"Watch this man," Miss Reba said again.

"Anything particular?" I felt my stomach cramping.

"Just look. See what this man does."

I did not see all of what the man did but I saw the beginning of it. He had held the pig's left ear and yanked the head to one side. The pig was making quick grunting noises. The two other pigs in the wood pen were also excited and making the same noises from deep in their throats. The two pigs shoved each other and pushed against the pen and kicked the dirty straw at the bottom of the pen. Wind carried the loose straw over the low wood railing and along the stone and sand ground. The pigs also kicked at the chickens and the chickens got more vocal than the pigs. One of the chickens had flapped its stubby wings very hard and it had leaped over the wood railing. This was when the Peruvian man reached under his orange and yellow poncho and retrieved a pistol. I think it was a German luger but I did not have a clear view. Then the man put the pistol to the pig's head and pulled the trigger. The shot was very loud and the tourists and the locals stopped what they were doing to look at the man and the pig. I felt Miss Reba's hands firm on my arms and she kept me pointed in the direction of the man.

"Remember what you see," she had said.

"…what's he doing?"

"Getting ready to cook the pig."

When the man had fired the shot, I saw the back of the pig's head come off, bits of it. I saw the blood spray and the pieces of flesh go across the tan stone and sand ground. The pig's legs had gone limp and the legs folded under the weight of its body.

I did not see the rest of it. My legs had folded under me, too. Blackness began at the periphery of my vision and brought a spiraling and complete darkness.

But before I fainted I'd had a brief image of Colonel Kohler. We were in his office after one of our dinners and he wanted to show me how to fire his pistol. I also saw the faces of two or three male prisoners in the barracks next to the Colonel's office. The prisoners watched us, their expressions wide-eyed and frozen like a deer in a bright light.

Fourteen

DALAL HAS TAKEN ME TO the *Gran Café de Paris* this morning for tea. The café has been around since the twenties and it was the first to take its business outside the Medina. In Tangier's International Zone days, the *Gran Café de Paris* had been a place for artists and writers, diplomats and spies. When Dalal tells me about this, she whispers the word "spies" as if it's a secret.

The café has plastic chairs and round tables outside and there are large shade trees nearby and a good view of everything that is going on around the *Place de France*. If you have your tea or coffee inside by the back window, you can look out at the port and the Mediterranean.

This morning Dalal and I are at a table near one of the trees.

"How is your mother?" I want to know.

Dalal's mother has breast cancer and she is a patient at the Mohamed V Hospital here in town. Dalal does not talk about her mother to me but I see her and her son take a taxi each morning and I am sure they stay at the hospital for many hours.

"Mama is not getting better."

"I'm sorry."

"She is an old woman," Dalal says. There is a shrug but she is not good at fatalism. Her voice has a sadness, an anxiousness about it. "What can I say? We all die of something."

"So, you are prepared?"

"Who is ever prepared for their mother to die?"

WHEN MY PARENTS die, I will remember how much they wanted to live. I'll remember them pleading with me to have dinner with Colonel Kohler. "What is a dinner?" they would say. "What difference could it make? He can help us. The Colonel can keep us alive." And in dreams I will see and hear the others suffering and praying and dying. I'll hear them shouting at us from their barracks while we slept in our house with the shutters and the glass in the windows.

"Think about us!" they would say. *Zamyslete se nad nami!*

178

"What about us!" *Co o nas?*

I have much darker feelings about my parents' deaths. I see myself fleeing everything my mother, father and I had gone through together.

In my fantasies, I am at their funerals. I witness the caskets sinking into the ground and I see the dirt pitched onto each casket. I imagine whatever history we endured buried with them. The faces, the days, the suffering and the praying.

I want the impossible. I want to see Theresienstadt disappear with my mother and my father and that will not happen, that will never happen.

Theresienstadt is a burial I will have to do.

"WHAT ARE YOU thinking?" Dalal says.

"...nothing."

"No, it is something."

"Ruminating. Nothing I want to bore you with."

"Well I won't push," she says.

Dalal is wearing western clothes today, a white high collar blouse and gray slacks. Both of us have on our brown hijabs and our sunglasses.

"You're a good friend," I say.

"I am here if you want to talk."

There were bees at the Café Hafa and there are

bees here, too. The bees crawl on the tables and sit on the rim of my tea glass. Two or three cars pass as we talk but the streets and the café are practically empty. This is Ramadan and no one should be at a café or a restaurant during daylight hours. Dalal is here to keep me company and talk but she is not drinking tea. Once in a while she waves away the bees from my tea glass like they were an annoyance without a sting. The people at the café are mostly tourists or they have that tourist look, the hats, the white tennis shoes, the cameras. There are couples, there are mothers and fathers and children.

It's the local men who are absent.

You will seldom see the likes of Dalal and me at a café; two women sitting alone is far too provocative. The men view us and women like us with suspicion. They are constantly on the lookout for women doing what we ought not to do and what we ought not to do is a long and tedious list invented by men. These men are forever vigilant and ready for violations. They wait for the scheming woman, the betrayer, the humiliator. Cafés are the fraternity houses of older men. It's the men who frequent the cafés and drink the tea and the coffee and smoke the cigarettes. It's the men who enjoy gossip and play backgammon.

But today the men are in the mosques and praying. They ask for guidance and forgiveness. They eat before sunrise and eat after sunset and in between that the praying is passionate and ceaseless.

"You follow Ramadan?" I say to my friend.

"I am a Muslim."

"No eating or drinking?" I say.

"Until sunset, yes."

"Then what?"

"I prepare the evening meal for my son and I," Dalal says. "I also pray during the day but at home. And I do good deeds. This year my good deeds are caring for my mother. I spend much time with her, seeing to her needs."

"So, you are a religious person?"

Dalal shuts her eyes for a moment and shakes her head.

"I try to do what I am supposed to do but I am not a perfect person." Dalal uses her middle finger to press her sunglasses to the bridge of her nose. "I have doubt in my heart, I am ashamed to say. I have been beaten for this. More than once, I have been beaten. My husband Ahmed, may his soul be blessed, he did not know what to do with me. 'How can you shame our family?' that was his question to me. I was not the wife he wanted. 'How can you shame our village?' But what could I say? I did not feel the things people felt. I have never seen the miracles people have seen."

"I also have this problem," I say.

"But you're an American."

"America is a very religious country."

"I did not mean any disrespect."

"That's the curse of the faithful," I say and smile.

Dalal waves the bees away from the top of my glass. She does not look at anything but the table and the tea. Then she tells me, "I once said to my husband, 'We are the only animals who fret about ourselves.' I had said to him, 'I believe it is terrifying to think that all we have is each other.' This why we invented God, to take care of us, to protect us. That was the first time he beat me. But I have not changed my mind."

Clouds have moved inland from the Atlantic and the clouds are at first a thick sulfur yellow and then they grow bigger and darker. Finally, the rain comes slow, steady. The *place* sign is attached to a metal extension above us and we can feel the wind and smell the ocean but we do not have to worry about getting wet.

"You are like me," I say.

"Pity you."

"No, pity them."

Dalal puts a manicured forefinger to her lips and looks at the other tables to see if anyone is listening. It is funny how friends meet. We have a sense of each other before we speak.

How can this be?

Many people I knew made excuses for God. That had been especially true in Theresienstadt. "God is testing us," they would say. "This is like God telling Abraham to bring his only son to the mountain. 'Sacrifice your son for me,' God tells him. 'Give me your most precious reason to live and I will know you adore me.' What makes this any different?" they'd say to one another.

The other side of the argument was this, "If there is a God, do you think we would be here? Are you crazy? What's wrong with you?" That was the Wake up and Smell the Coffee argument.

"I am glad you're my friend," Dalal says.

"Me, too." And I mean it.

IT'S HARD TO find a friend. My last good friend was Posie Frost who was my only roommate at VCU in Richmond. Posie was Chinese or her mother was Chinese and her father was something else but I don't remember what, exactly. Irish, I think. Sometimes when people from different races get together they produce these amazing hybrids. And that was Posie. Slim, pale, wonderful asian hair that I would kill for; she was a beauty and did not know it. Her hair was especially long and lovely and had a reddish tint to it. Both Poise and I were very shy so we got along well. Once again, invisible people at peace with their own kind.

Her parents were big into marijuana and on Saturday afternoons Poise would go home – Lenexa, if I'm remembering right—and she'd bring back a plastic baggie full of weed. I never smoked any of it myself but I didn't have to. All I had to do was be in the room and breathe.

Posie was the one who found me in the bathroom after I had cut my wrists over my ex-fiancée, the hideous Michael Sheetz, may God have mercy on his soulless hollow being. She had called the rescue squad and had stayed with me until they arrived. You would have thought one of her parents had cut a wrist instead of a roommate. But I will never forget her tears, the way she rocked me in her lap. I was shocked. The idea of someone caring about me like that.

THE RAIN IS coming down now. It is a soft dripping noise and there is steam rising from the downtown streets of Tangier, the *Place de France*. Dalal and I are watching the rain from beneath the metal covering outside the Gran Café de Paris. The sidewalks are slick with it and have a polished marble look.

The rain also brings the fresh smell of pine and ocean.

"You are very quiet today," Dalal says.

"I did not sleep last night."

"I have offended you," she says.

"Oh, no. Never."

"Are you sure?"

Dalal has removed her sunglasses to examine my face. She has a worried look, maybe curiosity more than worry. I keep my own sunglasses on but I give her my best smile. I do not want to talk about the Colonel. I want to talk about something light, a cheerful something.

"Aabid has to have those boots," I say.

"Ah the cowboy boots, yes." Dalal's eyes widen and she also smiles. The tension in her face disappears. "That's all he talks about, those boots. He says he will polish the boots every night. He says he will go to bed in the boots. I say to him, 'Aabid, you know you have manners. Have I not taught you what to do with shoes? You will get the sheets dirty. I do not have money to pay the hotel extra to clean the sheets.' But this does no good."

"He wants me to take him," I tell her. "He probably thinks he can get away with more if I take him. He's so charming."

"Aabid is a salesman, is he not?"

"Oh, God, yes."

"Boys and men beguile us."

"I am afraid I will lose him."

"I have tried to lose him many times," Dalal says and hides a quick laugh with her fingertips. "Perhaps I should say, I have wanted to lose him many times. Oh, I love him, certainly I love him. The boy is my life. But he can wear out the most blessed of us."

"Well when you visit your mother some evening soon, you must let me take him to the Medina to get his boots. Aabid will be a very happy son. Maybe we should go in the daylight. What do you think?"

"My Mother likes to see me in the evening," Dalal says. "She has her treatments in the morning. Aabid knows how to survive. You would not know it to look at him but Aabid is a good runner. He grew up with a very angry father. A boy who can outrun an angry father can survive anything."

The wind has slanted the rain and rushes it through the branches of the trees near the café. I feel its dampness on my face, the cool air. Summer showers can come and go very quickly in Tangier. Having a glass of mint tea and talking to a friend is a decent way to wait it out.

"I think your business is troubling you," Dalal says.

"I think you're right."

"Can you quit your business?"

"I wish it were possible," I say.

"People quit things. Why can't you quit?"

"I'd be worse off," I say. That's the truth.

"I know how that is." Dalal's face and her hijab are damp from the rain, too. We are sitting beneath a jutting metal overhead but it cannot completely block the angle of the rain. We are now the only ones sitting outside the café. Dalal is saying, "I do not want to see my mother die but I cannot walk away from her. I would never forgive myself. Isn't that the same?"

"Yes, something like that."

Miss Reba once said that Colonel Kohler stole my faith.

"I do not know how he did this," Reba had said. "But we will find out. We will get this back for you. You cannot go through your life so wounded."

At first this did not make sense.

I became a witness in a lot of ways. I had seen people getting off the trains, the cattle cars. I saw the corpses they had stampeded, the sick ones who had died on the journey, the ones who had suffocated. Survivors fled the trains. Women dropped their babies and the people running behind them stepped on these babies and crushed them. What God lets babies be crushed? Twenty to fifty thousand people a day were marched through the woods at Auschwitz and were stripped naked and murdered. Twenty to fifty thousand a day and more. More. Who lets that happen? Seriously. Who lets that happen? "Oh no, no. God does not deal with that," the debate goes. "God does not interfere."

But he parted the Red Sea. He let his son walk from the tomb.

We need God so much we will make any and all excuses, give any and all reasons. We have argued this in Theresienstadt, Auschwitz, Majdanek, Sobibor, Belzec, Treblinka, and so on and so on. And what do we have when it is done? I will tell you what I thought at thirteen and what I think now. We have a God who does magic tricks but does not help innocent people escape the gas chambers and the ovens. That's what we have, what we have always had. We need the idea of God too much and we are willing to forgive that idea too much.

"This is not the problem," Miss Reba had said. Then she said, "We will take the ayahuasca together, you and me. We will open the gate."

I had kept all this from my mind until Tangier.

Fifteen

"I AM SO VERY GLAD we are going to the market, Auntie Liora." The boy is very adamant about this. He is adamant about everything. Sweet but persistent, that's how I would describe him.

I am not his real aunt. I do not think I am anybody's aunt, not anybody I know. But my friend Dalal thought some type of respect was in order and I did not want Aabid calling me Doctor or Missus.

"You really want those cowboy boots," I say.

"You are an intelligent woman."

"It's my curse."

This is a twelve-year-old who wears gray suits with short pants and dark knee socks and talks like he is thirty.

Aabid and I are walking the *Rue de la Kasba,*

not far from the Medina and the market. We're doing what the Spanish call the *paseo*, the evening promenade. This a very popular thing to do in Tangier. Tourists and locals also like spending evenings at the cafés along *Place de France* and *Place de Faro*. There are good views of the port and the straits from these cafés. One can have a glass of sweet mint tea and watch the lights from the ships on the Mediterranean.

Dalal has gone to see her mother in the hospital. The mother's cancer is not responding to treatment and Dalal is very worried. Dalal does not want her mother to die but she is not naïve and she's preparing herself for the worse. I am keeping my promise to spend an hour or so with her son.

"I want the boots with the silver toes," Aabid says. His face is round and tan and he has his mother's delicate features, the chin, the long eyelashes. He is overweight but nice looking and would be a handsome boy if he lost fifteen or twenty pounds. "Can you picture me with such boots?" he says.

"Your friend Khalid would be very envious."

"Khalid?" The boy looks at me as if I have insulted him. "Khalid is not my friend," he says "How can you say this, Auntie? You are a doctor. You are an educated woman. A woman who has a profession worthy of respect. People admire you, do they not?"

"Some, I suppose." They are obviously misguided.

"Khalid is a plague."

"You talk about Khalid all the time."

"The way a general talks of his enemies."

"I think you like him," I say, half teasing.

"I would rather be a friend to spiders."

"You should make friends with your enemies," I say. I am wearing the brown hijab Dalal gave me and the wind from the ocean trembles the material against my ears and beneath my neck. I tell Aabid, "An enemy who becomes a friend is with us for life."

I do not know if that is true. But if it is not true it should be true.

"Who would want such a horrible friend, Auntie?" the boy says. "I do not understand. He is a far better enemy."

THE EVENING IS early and the sun is almost gone. Orange and pink streaks hang in the sky and the clouds are full and have a sulfury yellowish tint to them. Puffed and beautiful clouds. It's a perfect evening, what I have come to expect in Tangier. The wind from the Atlantic bring bits of sand with it and I feel stings on my neck and face. I have no idea what it is like in Casablanca or Marrakech but in Tangier the wind is always gritty.

Ramadan goes on but the fasting is done for another day. Candle flames can be seen in the minarets and in the distance are drums and flutes and lots of talking and laughter. During Ramadan, many people have breakfast before dawn and have another meal after sunset. The evening is a very pleasant relief.

"We must be quick," I tell Aabid.

"I am exceptionally quick."

"You know the shop?" I have my hand on his shoulder and I am looking down at his hair. It's cut very short, no more than bristles. "You know what I'm saying? The place where they make the boots?"

"I know the shop," he says. Now there is excitement in his voice. No doubt the boy has imagined wearing his silver toed boots and walking back and forth in front of his nemesis Khalid, glorying in the other boy's envy. "Mama and I come here all the time to visit grandmother. The shop is not far from here," he says. "We can be very quick."

"And careful, Aabid. You know how it can be in the Medina at night."

"You are like Mama."

"She's a wise woman."

"Sometimes she is wise," Aabid says. He is walking with me but he has a slow gait. His head is down and he is counting his dirham. This is the third time. And as Aabid counts, he says, "Sometimes Mama can become more fearful than necessary. This is the fate of women. They are filled with anxiousness and worry. And they love too much. This is not what men do. Men are better at the world."

"Who told you that?"

"It is known."

"Known does not mean true."

I am not surprised at what I am being told but I do not care for it. Children will remember the foolish talk of their parents and the friends of their parents. The children who do not get a university education or get away from the neighborhood for a while and live with other cultures and other points of view are doomed to carry on the talk and the ideas of the people who raised them. Children need to get away. It makes living in the world easier for everybody.

"My father believed this was true about women," the boy says.

"Your mother loves you enough to protect you."

"You do not think I know?"

"I am just reminding."

"I do not need reminding, Auntie." Aabid has folded his money and he pushes the bills into the front pocket of his gray short pants. Then he looks at me and says, "I am fortunate to have such a mother. She saved me from my father when he would feel bad and become angry. I was also very sick when I was a baby. I had diphtheria and I would bleed from my nose and could not breathe. This is what Mama said. She said, 'Aabid, your skin was very blue and you did not stop coughing.' She said, 'You would cry when you swallowed and you had a terrible fever. I also cried, Aabid,' she told me. 'I did not want to lose my precious boy.' If it was not for Mama, I would have died."

"I am glad your mama knew how to get you better."

"She is very good with treatments."

"You are a lucky boy." Dalal was born to be a mother.

I FOLLOW AABID into the Medina. We are on the *Rue Ben Abdessadek* and it is lovely and winding and old. There is the smoky aroma of cooking beef coming from the food vendors a block or two away. I remember Dalal's warning about women walking in the old city at night and I start feeling anxious. I am thinking, here I am and I'm walking the old city at night and I'm doing this with her son. Aabid needs to get his cowboy boots with the silver toes and leave. And I tell him that.

"We cannot stay here," I say.

"Do not worry, Auntie."

"No, no. Don't give me that auntie business," I tell him. "I am not one of your women who worry too much. I am not the jokes of men."

"I did not mean to insult you."

"Just listen to me, Aabid." I kneel down in front of him and hold his arms and wait until he looks at me. "Most of the people here are good people. But the ones with problems come out at night. Problems always come out at night. When men are hungry and tired and they are caught in a month of prayer, some of these good men are not themselves. Do you understand?"

"I am not a stupid boy, Auntie Liora."

"Nobody's calling anybody stupid."

"I know this is a difficult time for women."

"Hey. Don't give me that."

I see a man in a wheelchair being pushed by another man. The man doing the pushing wears a fedora and has a blond braid. They are across the street by the stalls, a few yards ahead of us. It is Colonel Kohler and Willem. I am so fascinated to see the old man in the Medina that I quit talking to Aabid for a moment and watch them. I can't see the Colonel's face but his head is cocked to the right and he is leaning to the right in his chair. This is the aftermath of a stroke, or so I am thinking.

The Colonel points to a black and gold ceramic vase in one of the stalls. Willem bows to the old man and I almost expect him to click his heels together. The nephew has turned to the street vendor. Willem snaps his fingers to get the vendor's attention. The vendor's stall is lit by an oil lantern. Light wavers in the breeze from the ocean and there is smoke coming from the open glass of the lantern. Then Willem and the vendor argue, I presume it's about the price of the vase. Now the Colonel dismisses Willem and the vendor with a wave of his hand and motions to the nephew. I can hear the anger in the Colonel's voice but I cannot hear his words. Willem's response to this surprises me. He stands in front of the Colonel with his hands folded and looking at the ground. Willem is like a child being scolded. Who can believe this is the same young man who beats up on his wife?

AABID TUGS ON the hem of my blouse for attention. The boy is still talking to me about how difficult it is for women to manage lives.

"…it's what is known," He is saying again.

"You will stop this talk about women," I say. There is a sharpness to my voice and I feel bad about it but it must be said. Aabid and I are putting

196

too much on the line for cowboy boots, I know
that, and I am putting too much on the line to win
a twelve-year old boy's approval. I know that, too.
But we are here and we will do this and go. I say to
him, "If it's a difficult time for women, Aabid, it will
be more than a difficult time for little boys. Okay?
You may find yourself alone and that is not what
you want, believe me. It's all the worried women
who keep our sons from harm."

"I, I am sorry." He is looking at the ground.

"You're a good boy," I say and kiss his forehead.
When I do that Aabid puts his arms around me. I
melt, absolutely melt. I have never felt anything like
that. "…okay, that's good, thank you." Why does
this embarrass me? "Let's get your cowboy boots
and get out of here," I whisper. I am stunned by
what a simple hug from a boy can do. I can barely
hear my words.

"Yes, Auntie."

WE ARE IN *Le Petit Socco*, the little square, though
not by the usual route, the one Dalal wrote down
for me a few days ago. Most people start at the
Grand Socco, the main city square, and go through
the ancient keyhole-looking archway that leads to

the *Rue de la Kasbah*. This is followed by a right turn onto the *Rue des Siaghines* and at the end of that street is the market.

Many cafés are here. In the days when Tangier was an international zone, drugs and people were sold and smuggled in the Medina. Prostitution was a way to make good money. A writer could walk the streets and fill a book or two. Things have changed today. 1974 is not like the 1920s or the 1950s. But what was here then is here now. I think people are just smarter about it.

The sky has become dark but I can see a sliver of moon above the rooftops and there are stars. The smell of food is close, meat cooking and smoking in the small shops and the cafés. The streets of the old city are very narrow and curved. The apartments are above the shops and the streets are lighted only by lamplight. It is easy to get lost in the shadows. I try to keep Aabid in my view but he is short and very quick and knows the area.

"Slow down," I call to him.

"Hurry, Auntie!" He shouts this without turn-ing around.

"You must slow down."

But the boy is not having that. He is bent on buying those cowboy boots with the silver toes. I have never felt more helpless and I start to run after him. I am a very good runner but the market place has many people and Aabid is better than I am at weaving through the crowd. Do not get me wrong. I am doing very well. It's not that I am all that far behind him. But I keep saying, "Excuse me" to people. And, "Pardon me." I am doing a lot of smiling and nodding and trying my best not to offend anyone and this is throwing me off my game. I still see Aabid moving through the shadow and the light. His puffy bare legs are going a lot faster than I would have thought they could go.

"Wait for me!" I say. Yell it, actually.

The boy is not answering me.

He is running faster than he needs to and I am sure he's caught in his fantasies of silver toed boots and the sweet and painful look of his friend Khalid.

"WHAT ARE YOU doing?" a man says. "Why are you here?"

I am startled into silence, a second or two.

"My boy is lost," I tell him.

The man is near a shadowed beige wall. I smell something sweet coming from him, perhaps soap, perhaps aftershave. Then the man steps toward me and into the weak yellow light of the shops and the apartments. He is tall and slender and wears jeans and a red and blue striped polo shirt. The remarkable thing about the man is that he is so average, his dark short hair, the start of a beard. There are many men like this man. Or I think I have seen many men like this man. But I am a stranger here and a stranger cannot see the differences in a group that is new and unknown. What we see first are the similarities of a group. What we see later are the differences.

It's the edge to his voice I don't trust. He is angry and I do not know why. No, that's not true, I do know why. This is exactly what my friend Dalal told me to avoid, the old city at night, the fast tempers of hungry men. I am what he does not like, what gets him anxious, a woman alone.

Worse still, an American woman alone.

"You should not be here," he says.

"I have to find my boy." I hear my own urgency.

"What are you?"

"I, I…what do you mean?" I don't know what he wants from me.

"You are American. Isn't that what you are?"

"I was born in Prague."

"You have an American accent."

I have never thought that until now. I have an American accent. What can I say? I think about my past too much and I do not think about my present at all. I have ignored what has become a part of me, I am an American.

"…Yes okay," I say. "I'm an American."

"You are not welcome."

The people of Tangier have always accepted other cultures, other religions. This acceptance is at the heart of Tangier. It's why so many people from so many places come here to find a home. But this is the month that feelings get very raw. People are hungry and irritable and want to protect their faith. People like me who don't have the same faith are viewed as being against the faithful. This is the month where it is difficult to tolerate anyone who is not doing what you are doing, fasting when you are fasting, eating when you are eating, sleeping when you are sleeping. This is the month where it is difficult to tolerate people who do not believe what you believe.

"I only want to find my boy," I say.

"You will leave now."

"Not without my boy, I won't."

I'm arguing with this man. Who argues with a crazy person? People who argue with a crazy person are crazy themselves. Who does that? But I'm feeling very stubborn and I know this is not the feeling I should express to a man who is stronger than I am and does not like women and Americans. If he knew I was a Jew, he'd become apoplectic. I also realize my hands are on my hips and I am meeting the man's angry look with a look of my own. More

than that, I *want* to keep my hands on my hips.
But I think better of it and take a breath and relax
my arms. I look down the narrow street. It's full of
shadows and lamplight. People are walking through
the Socco, locals mostly. No one is watching us.

"This is a sacred time," he says.

"I am not bothering you." I try to keep my words
calm and even. I do not want to stir up whatever bees
are in his head. "My boy is lost," I say. "I will find
him and leave."

"What sort of mother loses a child?"

I'M ABOUT TO tell him that none of that is his concern
but I feel a hand on the back of my neck and I am
yanked away and thrown to the ground. It happens
very fast. The power of it amazes me. Even as I am
falling I am amazed by it. The side of my head hits the
street and there is pain and blood. I touch above my
right eye and look at my fingers. It's not a lot of blood
but it's enough and I know my eye will be bruised.

"This will be a bad night for you."

I turn to the voice and recognize the man who
threw me. It's Willem with his tan fedora and his
blond braid. At first I think he is telling me *this will
be a bad night for you* but he is saying that to the
man near the beige wall.

Willem up-close is much bigger than I had thought, his arms, his shoulders, his hands. He isn't a tall man but he isn't a man who needs to be tall. Willem is also by himself. I am guessing the Colonel is back in his own apartment.

The man who'd ordered me to leave the Medina is now on the ground and being kicked by Willem. His knees are to his chest, hands over his head. Blood seeps between the fingers. Willem is very quiet but he does not stop kicking him. The man is quiet, too. Willem grabs him by his red and blue Polo shirt and pushes him down the street and the man stumbles then gets his balance and goes into the shadows.

This is not the end of it; I know it right away. I am pulled up and pressed against the wall and Willem's hand is on my throat. His eyes are very blue, very cold. He holds a knife in his right hand, the point to my neck. The blade is thin and long and reflects the lamplight.

"My marriage is not your business," he says.

"...I have to find my friend's child."

Willem releases me and folds the blade of the knife into its handle and returns the knife to his pocket. My legs are no good and I am lying on the street. He tosses a canary yellow envelope next to me. The envelope has my name on written in a neat black ink script.

"The Colonel wrote this?" I say and hear the weakness in my voice.

"He dictates. I'm the one who writes."

"…thank you."

"Just keep your word," Willem says.

"My word? I, I…don't understand."

"What you said to my wife. Tell my uncle, that's our deal. Tell him what a thoughtful guy I am."

Ah, I remember. Willem gets me a dinner with the Colonel, and I tell the old man how he's a fine, deserving nephew.

"You eat, you go," Willem says.

"Let me put your mind at ease," I say. "I want nothing from your uncle. Do you understand? There's nothing he has – nothing he would ever have – that I'd want." I turn to leave but I stop and turn again to look at him. He has his uncle's eyes; I see that now, so blue, so cold. Then I say, "Who knows, Willem, maybe you'll become a rich man sooner than you think."

Sixteen

THE RIGHT SIDE OF MY forehead is swollen and has a big purplish bruise from my fall in the Medina. I also have a two-inch abrasion, though it looks worse than it is. And the aspirins I took aren't helping. But thank God I got Aabid and his new cowboy boots back to his mother.

It's now two thirty-two in the morning and I'm sitting up in bed with the small nightstand lamp on and rereading the Colonel's letter.

The fourth or fifth time, I don't know which.

My dear Liora,
Welcome to Tangier! It's such a marvelous city,

*don't you think? So old, so charming. This is partic-
ularly true of the Medina. One imagines spies and
disreputables prowling about its narrow streets at
night, selling and buying all manner of things. This
is truly the first time I have ever felt at home. That's
the magic of Tangier, isn't it? Patient, mysterious,
seductive, Tangier is the home that waits for us to
find it.*

*Have you walked Atlantic Beach? Have you
gone to the Café Hafa and had a glass of their lovely
mint tea and looked out at the Mediterranean? I have
done that but I did not like the bees. The way they
gather on the rim of the tea glass for the sugar – who
can tolerate such a thing! I also have no patience for
these vendors. They are like the Jews with all their
bargaining, a dirham here, two dirhams there. I will
have none of it. (Please excuse the Jewish remark but
you of all people would understand what I mean,
darling Liora.)*

*I am also displeased with the way people here
disregard time. They will show up fifteen or twenty
minutes late for a meeting and think nothing of it.
It's unbelievable! But perhaps precision is a genetic
fault of mine, a German trait. Our trains run on
time. Our meetings take place on time. We do not
appreciate tardiness in any form. If we say we will
complete a task at a specific moment, it's completed
at that moment. That is our German mind; that is*

our German soul. We take pride in doing what we say we will do when we say we will do it.

It's the German way.

Also, the Muslims here pray far too much. They are like the Jews, are they not? You know it is the truth. And you and I have never been afraid of telling the truth, have we? (You have always been my gateway to the Jews, darling Liora.) Every time we turn around a Jew is on his knees praying. You can certainly testify to that peculiar fact. The Muslims are no different, really. Morning, noon or night, there is this incessant praying. God must shake His head and wonder when He will get peace. "Here they go again," God says. "Here come the Jews. Here come the Muslims. Pray, pray, pray. They are driving me crazy," God says.

I will be the first to admit how well the Jews have done since the war. I will also admit I am not surprised. Resiliency! I used to say this to my staff all the time. "Look how the Jews are surviving," I would tell them. "They cling to life regardless of its terms." My staff and I were both stunned and amused.

What is that clever American saying? Lemonade out of lemons? That's the Jews. (How the Jews survived and prospered has never stopped being a subject of conversation and wonder.) My comical friend, Bering, used to say, "As long as two Jews are *left to procreate, we are in trouble!" A very gifted jokester, you must agree. We would all laugh at Heir Bering's humor but we knew it was the truth.*

The party denied the Jews their Jewish businesses and access to our banks. We denied them jobs in manufacturing and in the cattle market. We refused to pay our debits to Jewish creditors; we foreclosed on their mortgages. And that was only the beginning of it. Yes, we did all these things and more (why I tell you what you already know is a mystery, darling Liora, but I do want you to know I know it, too).

But the Jew was not to be dissuaded!

I can hear you saying that now. I can see you with your skinny arms crossed and your chin jutting out, such a defiant little thing, such bravado. The Jews may have been passive but they were never dissuaded. And some say they were not passive. Some say this is what happens to cultured and civilized people who have experienced years of being demoralized, stripped of their humanity. (I know you know this but again I want you to know your Colonel is aware of these arguments.)

If you do know that about your Colonel, then you must also know how I and I alone protected you and your family from our little corner of the war.

It was not by chance that I picked my Liora and

her mother and father. It was not a camp lottery. I was not blindfolded and throwing darts at a board. I did not take a name from a hat or have a best essay contest. This very much had to do with my affection for you. No, let us be honest. This very much had to do with my love for you. This is true and I am not the least embarrassed by such a wonderful fact. You were (and you are) my interest of interests, my obsession of obsessions.

Yes, it's true.

Rightly or wrongly, there was nothing fair about choosing you and not someone else. (But who ever heard of a war that was fair? A "fair" war, what a joke, what an oxymoron!)

I saved your family from the trains going east. I saved you and yours from the gas of Auschwitz and Buchenwald. If I may be bold, I would say your life after Theresienstadt was my gift to you.

And I gave this gift lovingly, willingly.

But what of you, darling Liora? How many years has it been since last we were together? Twenty-nine? Thirty? Twenty-nine, I believe.

I must confess, for me no time has passed. I remember you as young enough to cause embarrassment but not regret. I remember you as a partner in a hell that neither one of us could escape. What comfort you gave to your Colonel? That lovely face, those long delightful legs, that unafraid attitude in *the midst of a world overwhelmed by fear. I believe to this very day that we were each other's salvation. I know you were mine.*

I have never married. I have never had children. I do not know the joy of sharing my life and relying on the love and the kindness of another. Nor will I see that shared life bloom in the faces of my children. Nor will I know what it is like for my children to have children. These things, these priceless things, have been lost to me forever or, perhaps more realistically, I have had the misfortune to confuse the priceless and the temporary, what is lasting and what gave me momentary relief.

I have had a life of illnesses and passions beyond my control. But I think I have always wanted what others have wanted. And I have wanted that with you. Darling Liora. And I still do. There is not a day in these last twenty-nine or thirty years that I have not imagined your presence, imagined the dinners and the talks we once had, imagined the kisses on my cheek that I forced out of you. Isn't it an unlikely finale, the Colonel and his lovely little Jewess?

Perhaps it is only human nature to travel a forbidden road. I cannot tell you the many fellow officers who have not had a drink of cognac or two and rhapsodized about the dark eyed Jewish girls.

We will have dinner, you and I. Tomorrow at 8

PM. My nephew, Willem, will tell you the place and give you directions. One cannot be too careful, even in Tangier. And I know the clock will strike and I will hear a knock on the door. Isn't this you, darling Liora? You have the soul of a Jew but the mind of a German.

We will have peas and mashed potatoes. And the piece de resistance, the roasted chicken, of course. Your very favorite. (Did you think I would ever forget?) And I will prepare it as I have always prepared it for you, salted and peppered and glazed in butter.

Your Colonel waits for you,
K.P. Kohler

Seventeen

IT'S 5:34 IN THE AFTERNOON and my dinner with Colonel Kohler is at eight. I have already showered and washed my hair. Willem has given me the address and directions. It's the Hotel Mamora on the *Rue Mokhtar Ahardan*. I must enter the Medina through the port side and walk down the *Rue de la Marine* to get there. This is a thirty-room hotel that has a view of the Mediterranean and a good breeze in many of the rooms. Dalal tells me it's an older hotel that has a damp sea odor and some of the rooms do not have toilets.

Embarrassing as it is, I am now thinking about what I am going to wear and how I am going to act. What do I want from this old man?

Only release, I think. I would like release.

I have also folded the plastic bag containing the dress and shoes I had taken from my parents' attic into a big leather handbag that has a shoulder strap, my long ago present from the Colonel. The dress and black patent leather shoes seem so fragile and childlike now.

Half of my life is spent getting ready for something.

I wipe the steam from the bathroom mirror with the sleeve of my terry cloth robe and study myself, my eyes, my mouth, my presentation. I have a new and smaller bandage over the abrasion above my right eye. What can I say? It is a presentation; I am being truthful. The wounded soldier-waif look. I try different expressions of disinterest. I say to the mirror, "Yes, Colonel, I am here but I am not sure I want to be here." I am thirteen years old again and haughty. "Look at you in that wheelchair. What can you do to me now?"

THINGS HAVE CHANGED.

And what has changed is what I have recalled, the parts of myself that have come back to me thanks to Miss Reba. It's what her friendship gave to me. Finding Colonel Kohler has taken time but I know what I need to do, what I must put into practice.

Miss Reba gave me back my memory, my life.

I had tried burying that life in Theresienstadt but what we feel and do always has to come with us. Burying your life never works out.

I had forgotten about Miss Reba and I walking through the Sunday market at Picas. I'd forgotten the wind coming down into the village through the Sacred Valley. The wind came in hard and beat about the Spring ice and the stones of the Pisaqa, the Intihuatana, the Q'allaqasa, the Kinchiracay, what was left of the Incas.

This was in 1959, the week I had started packing my things to go back to the states. During our walk about the market, Miss Reba had gripped my arms and turned me toward the man and the dark wood pen that had held the pigs and the chickens. I watched the man take a Lugar from under his orange and yellow poncho, and shoot the pig.

"Remember what you see," she'd said.

I had seen the shooting and lost consciousness right away. I despised myself for that. I was not a weak person. I'd seen the extremes in men and women, how we treated each other. The camps brought out the best and the worst in us. The petty envies, the stealing, the relief that a friend was being tortured instead of one's self, the whispers made to the guards about this prisoner or that prisoner, it never stopped. A man shooting an animal should not have affected me in such a way.

＊ ＊ ＊

THE NEXT MORNING Miss Reba came to my hut. The two small windows and the open turquoise door let in the sunshine and the chill of the wind. This was a wind we could hear. She had a clay bottle filled with ayahuasca. Reba also had a tan wool blanket for me and what she called the Brugmansia or sacred tobacco, the Mapacho.

"I can't do this," I said.

"I will be with you."

"I don't care."

"Do you really want to live in a mystery?"

I did not understand what she meant, to live in a mystery. I did not see any mystery. I thought this was mumbo-jumbo shaman talk. Like The Gate. Like the Call to Awaking. Like Death and Rebirth. I saw myself as a person who had gone through bad times and I saw myself as lucky to have escaped the bad times. There was no good reason to repeat what I had escaped.

"You must step away from yourself," Miss Reba said. She was sitting next to me on the straw mat I used for my bed. Her arms were crossed in front of her and pressed to her chest. She had her pipe in the corner of her mouth but it was unlighted. She said, "You are an anthropologist. This doesn't interest you?"

Miss Reba is a Daime or ayahuasca shaman of the religious sect called the Santo Daime. This group was founded in the thirties in the Amazonian state of Acre by Raimundo Irineu Serra. Santo Daime is a mix of Catholicism, Kardecist Spiritualism, South American Shamanism, and African animisms. The ayahuasca had been named "Daime" by Irineu, Portuguese for "give me." Santo Daime had no written text at its start. What they did have were hymns or *trabalhos* and the congregation sang the hymns for many hours. The hymns had to do with love, harmony with nature and one another, that sort of thing.

"This Colonel keeps working on you," Miss Reba said. She was lighting her pipe with a wood match but the draw was giving her trouble and she tapped the bowl with the end of the match to loosen the shreds of dried caapi. "Even when the Colonel is not there he is working on you," she said and lighted the pipe again. "Do you want that to be your fate?"

I DID TAKE the ayahuasca. We had shut the door to the hut and I had lain on my straw mat. Miss Reba covered me with the tan wool blanket. She had given me a shot glass worth of the ayahuasca

216

in a tiny clay cup and she had swallowed the same amount in the same cup. These vines and the leaves are boiled for many hours and it is the boiled runoff that is the true ayahuasca. The texture of the drug is thick and brown and gritty. Its taste is similar to rotting fruits but with a slight prune flavor. Before Reba gave me the shot glass she had smoked the *Mapacho* and blew the smoke on the ayahuasca to bless it.

To be honest I did not notice any difference inside myself. I waited and waited but did not feel anything…unusual. This was over an hour, I am sure. I had even said to Miss Reba, "Shouldn't I take more of it? Nothing is working."

"That would be a mistake."

"But it's been a very long time."

"Be patient," she said.

"Why not take more? Every person is different."

"People have done so and regretted it."

"In what way?" I did not get this.

"You do not want to find out."

Miss Reba was right. The ayahuasca does not care whether you are ready for it or not. It comes to you when it decides to. That was what I'd learned. It comes in its own time, its own manner, in the abrupt full rising of its readiness. When the aya-huasca showed itself it was a rumble and a crack in the earth. It shook me into a deep and uncanny feeling of well-being. The feeling was not anything a person would want to quit.

What I received were visions and not hallucina-tions. There were colors and some geometric shapes but the shapes and the colors came as static that flawed my visions. I could have sat in the center of it and just watched it unfold. Ayahuasca is the drug for academics, for social scientists and for graduate students who liked taking notes. I became the ulti-mate, absolute witness. My dream of dreams. Ha! With geometric static all around me, I watched my visions with fascination. There was a wonder in the fear of it. And that day at the market became clear, what the man and the pig had meant to me.

I watched the visions and I heard Miss Reba chanting the Icaros, the power songs of the shaman. These are chants used to speak to the spirits in the natural world, to heal the sick and to provoke cer-tain types of visions.

"Remember what you see," I heard Miss Reba tell me.

I WAS THE graduate student who stood in a shadowed corner and observed my thirteen-year-old self in Colonel Kohler's office. I remembered the building as ocher colored. It was surrounded by gray barracks. Windows were cut into the side of the walls of the barracks but the windows had no glass. Skull faces would appear and vanish in the windows. The prisoners wanted to know what was happening in the ocher colored building, what the Colonel was up to. I think they knew about me, too. They knew I spent time with him.

The Colonel always looked dapper. He had an ultra-scrubbed shine about him, hair slicked back beneath his cap, rimless glasses refusing to get in the way of an angular face.

I liked being here in his office better than I liked our house. I had started to hate the little house he had given to my family. I hated the house because it was in the center of the camp and the other prisoners hated it and hated us for living in it. The prisoners hated the clean white exterior, the shutters, the gingerbread trim, and the glass in the windows.

Who could blame them?

The prisoners yelled and cursed at us all the time. They did not want us to sleep in comfortable beds. They did not want us eating eggs and fresh fruits and vegetables. The prisoners hated our potbelly stove and the coal that burned in our stove and kept us warm. They called Mother and Father

Nazi lovers and worse, terrible names. Then the prisoners would yell at me to get out from the devil house while the getting was good. "Hurry now, you poor child," they'd call out. "There is still hope for you!"

"Wait until you see the dinner I've prepared," the Colonel said to me one late afternoon in his office.

I was wearing my silk dress with the crinolines. The dress had blue ribbons on it and the shoes matched the pale blue of the ribbons. All my family's clothing had been picked out by the Colonel. My father always wore nicely fitted suits and my mother had a different dress every day, selected from the large pile of clothes people left behind as they boarded the trains for the other camps. I thought my silk dress and the matching blue shoes were too pretty for me. I did not belong in clothes like that. My arms and legs were bony and pale. I also had bleeding sores and I was always afraid I would ruin everything.

"I do not like meat," I said. Too haughty, too foolish.

"No, no. This isn't meat."

"I don't like soups, either."

"Don't you think I know that?"

The Colonel listened to me and knew what I liked and what I did not like. I had to give him that.

I thought he knew more about me than my parents. He used to prepare dinners for us in a tiny kitchen in the back room of his office. The room had an oven and a refrigerator and a butcher's block.

Many times, he would give me a new dress and new shoes to wear at dinner. If I wanted to keep the new dress and shoes, I'd have to give him a hug and a kiss before I left the office. The hugs were brief and the kisses were tiny and light. I do not think my kisses were that good but the Colonel would always tell me how pleased he was and how much he liked them. I heard him do the same tiny sounds in his throat that he did when he walked about me for his inspections. I would feel him tremble, his legs, his arms. That made me tremble, too. I knew I'd made him feel something and I felt strong inside.

I could still hear Miss Reba's chanting the Icaros but the chanting was very far off. I thought it was coming from the gray barracks across from the Colonel's office. I remember wondering why the Nazis had decided to bring Miss Reba to Theresienstadt. There were other things, too. Once in a while, colors and shapes disrupted what was going on in the office.

"It smells wonderful," I said. The Colonel was a good cook, I had to admit that. "What is it?" I said. "Tell me what you are cooking. It smells like roasted chicken. Is that it? I'm right, aren't I?"

Colonel Kohler lighted one of his thin black cigars. He was sitting in the wood swivel chair, his polished boots crossed at the ankles, heels on the desk. His smile had not quit since I had entered the office. It had a glossy painted-on look. His face never tried anything beyond that smile. Sunlight came through the open window and reflected at the edges of his rimless glasses. He blew the cigar smoke toward the afternoon light and the smoke changed from white to gold.

"No keeping things from you," he said. "So lovely and so very smart. What a dangerous combination, darling."

Roasted chicken has always been my favorite. I will take roasted chicken over steak or lobster or what-have-you. I do not know why the Colonel thought these things were important enough to remember, my favorite foods, the dresses and shoes, the music I liked. I could walk into his office on, say, Friday and the music we had talked about on Thursday would be playing in the background. My father loved *Madame Butterfly*. He loved *La Boheme* and Giuseppe Verdi's *The Four Seasons*. Because father loved this music I loved it, too. But the Colonel never questioned me about such things. What is your favorite food? What is your favorite music? He heard my likes and dislikes in our talks and he remembered.

That was the stunning part for me. The man remembered. When he'd invite me into his office Verdi played, a dress and shoes waited. He took many chances and introduced me to new music and new foods I might like. He extrapolated, roasted duck and goose. The first time I heard Chopin's *Op. 28* was in Colonel Kohler's office, the first time I heard Carmen.

The Colonel had a beautiful record player, I do not know what type. It was a dark polished wood and it had the look of a smooth cube and he had the cube on a pedestal beside his desk. He would slip the record out of its jacket, the palms of his hands pressed to its rim. The cube was already opened by then and he'd place the record on the turntable. His fingers never touched the grooves, the disk itself. Before doing this he would study the record in the sunlight by his window and blow the dust from its black surface.

"You will love this," he would say.

"I'm no pushover."

"I know, darling. Don't you think I know?"

"I must be honest."

"…one of your charms."

I am thirteen years old and I am giving a Nazi shit. More than once I have thought about this and cringed at that thought. What was I thinking? Had I so little concern for my life and the lives of my mother and father? The man could have killed us for any reason or no reason. He could have killed us just to stop his boredom. This is true, believe me. I was a fly ready to be swatted. The Colonel did not need a reason to kill people. He killed people because this is what he did, a bit of self-indulgence, a whim. But in my defense, I thought he liked me giving him shit. He liked to see my courage. He liked the blindness of it, courage in the face of all odds. Insane courage. And the more insane it was the better he liked it and the more amused he found the person who did it. That was his personality. I am sure there was a line-in-the-sand for him, a line no one crossed but it was also a line no one could find and no one knew. Looking back, I'd been an emaciated motor-mouthed thirteen year old who by luck alone got through it all.

I was in Colonel Kohler's office and I was hearing Miss Reba chanting the Icaros. The chanting appeared then disappeared, but each time it did appear I had pulled back from my visit and reoriented as an observer. I believe the Icaros allowed me to keep the distance I needed to make sense of things. Along with Miss Reba's chanting there was the visible static from the drug. The bright colors and the geometric shapes would blink in an out. I did not know the analogy then but now I see it as a bad sixties music video. Occasionally I could feel the geometric shapes touch me.

"I hope you are hungry," the Colonel had said.

"I love the smell."

"I will serve you myself." He had actually clicked the heels of his boots together and gave me a little bow.

A table had been set up near his desk. The table was a small round pub table draped with a white linen cloth. Late afternoon sunlight came through the three office windows, the yellow light glittered with particles of dust.

The Colonel stood behind me and tied a white bib about my neck. He was very careful not to tie the bib too tight and asked me several times if it the bib was loose enough.

"I feel like a child," I said.

"You are a child, darling."

"So, you have dinner with children?"

"If they are beautiful, yes."

Somewhere during our dinner conversation, I had confessed that my secret name for him was Colonel Smiley. The Colonel was relighting a thin black cigar he had been holding between his index and middle fingers. He'd laughed and his laugh became a phlegmy cough.

"Oh, that's wonderful," he'd said. He laughed and coughed again.

"You're not angry?"

"What could be more wonderful?"

"You smile too much," I said.

"I do, yes. I do indeed."

There was a thick straw target by the window to the right. Sunshine slanted over it, the rich deep light that had begun the evening. The straw target had many bullet holes. This was where Colonel Kohler taught me how to shoot. He would hold my waist with one hand while his other hand kept my pistol balanced and directed at the target.

"You must have other feelings," I said. I was seated at the table and eating baby lima beans and recalling our target practice. "Or maybe you have a different life and different feelings."

"What if I am a happy person?"

"Nobody is that happy."

"You don't find life amusing?"

"You shoot people and smile," I said. The chicken was very good, very moist, with a caramelized skin and a sprinkling of pepper. I did not like thinking about the Colonel shooting people. But when I did think about it I could not let go of it. "I have seen you shoot prisoners," I said. "I saw you aim your pistol out that window and shoot into the barracks next door. I have seen you do it."

"It doesn't amuse you?"

"What do you mean?" I could not believe what I was hearing.

"The way people look before they die."

"No, it doesn't amuse me. How can you say that?"

"You are a troubling girl."

The Colonel blew a narrow line of cigar smoke into the sunlight and watched the smoke glitter and dissipate. The tobacco had a burnt chocolate smell. He did not quit his smile but I believe he was thinking about our talk and the shock I felt at hearing his words.

He shook his head and told me, "I have said this before but let me say it again. How can you get through this world with a heart like that? You are too young and your heart is too sweet."

After our dinner, I decided to help and I carried our plates and trays into the little kitchen behind his office. When I came back he had removed his Luger from its leather holster and was wiping the barrel with a folded handkerchief.

"Let's see if I taught you anything."

"I'm not feeling well."

"Come, come," he said and motioned me to him.

I had started to feel nauseated.

I could hear Miss Reba chanting again but she sounded very far away. For a second or two I had stepped back from all this and I remembered the purgative effect of the ayahuasca and I had wondered how long it would be before I began to vomit and shit.

My God. I did not want to embarrass myself.

The Colonel had given me the pistol. His hand was on my waist and his other hand steadied my arm. I fired a shot into the target and hit the edge of the red bullseye. "Very good," he whispered, his breath on my ear. I heard him breathing through his mouth. I smelled his cologne and the cigar smoke on his jacket. "…and again," he had said. I fired the pistol for the second time and got the bullet closer to the center of the small red circle. "Let's do something else," the Colonel said. His voice was soft and even and calm. Then he put his hand over my hand, his forefinger over the forefinger I was using to pull the trigger of the pistol. He shifted my arm toward the open window. With his forefinger on mine, he began shooting the pistol into the barracks next door.

I saw a woman get hit in the face with one of my bullets. I saw the man beside her lose the back of his head the way the pig lost the back of its head when the Peruvian man shot him. I saw both bodies disappear from the window of the barracks.

I had started to scream.

I remembered that now. I remembered Colonel K. P. Kohler holding my waist and I remembered myself screaming.

"Listen to you," he had said. I could feel the breath of his voice on my ear. "You are with me now," he'd said. "Now your heart is not so sweet."

Eighteen

IT IS CLOSE TO EIGHT and again I am by myself in the Medina. I hear Dalal's warning about women alone at night, especially during Ramadan. I am suspicious about why I put myself in this situation but I become suspicious only after I have entered the Medina through the port side. This is self-destructive behavior of the worst sort. I have tried to dress conservatively, a gray linen suit, my brown *hijab* Dalal bought me, the leather strap of my handbag hanging from my shoulder.

Now I am walking down the *Rue Mokhtar Ahardan* on my way to the Hotel Mamora and Colonel Kohler. I am probably stewing about my past crimes and looking for punishment.

"Late for the prom?" This is a voice I behind me.

"…Leon?"

"Don't be angry."

"ARE YOU FOLLOWING me?" I am relieved to see Leon Nauman but I will not tell him that. Certain people should never be encouraged.

"A hot number like you? Sure."

Already he's annoying.

I am about to tell Leon that I'm his employer and so on, my usual with him, but I quit the thought before it gets too out of hand. Instead I pat his shoulder. It's my compromise between encouragement and gratefulness.

"I brought you a gun," he says and touches the breast of his suitcoat.

"I don't need a gun."

"Just in case."

"The man is in a wheelchair," I say.

"He can't shoot you sitting down?"

"He invited me to dinner."

"One's got nothing to do with the other."

"Maybe you have a point, Leon." Why do I argue?

Silver light divides the shadows and its threads crisscross the streets. The night sky is clear and many stars and a thick slice of moon brings this light. Wind from the ocean comes over the walls and the roofs. Bits of sand whirls about us. I can hear the drums and flutes. Prayers are done now and most folks here are eating an evening meal at the food stands, they are talking and laughing.

"People can change their minds," Leon says. He means me having dinner with Colonel Kohler. "You don't think people can do that? Hey, let me tell you, people change their minds every day. They change their minds about who knows what, everything."

"What would be my reason?"

"That's what you're asking?"

"Yes, why cancel?"

Leon has bought himself a red Fez. He is wearing the Fez with a royal blue sports jacket and brown corduroys. He is a sixty-something person who has no anxiety about mixing his fashion statements.

"Let's think about how this man could hurt you," Leon says. He puts his arms about my waist and I sidestep away from it. "I've been thinking a lot about this. Maybe it's a mistake."

"God, please. Let's not go there."

"He could shoot you."

"Seriously, Leon, let's not."

"He could poison your food," Leon says. "We're talking dinner. He could poison your drink." Leon is using his fingers to count the ways the Colonel might kill me. "All I am saying is I am concerned about you. Are you listening? Don't think I don't know about these things.

"The man never hurt me. Why now?"

"There's always a first time," he says.

"Yes, I know."

"Look, I am giving an opinion," Leon says. He removes the red Fez and wipes his balding head with a handkerchief. "You think I'm a kid? You think I don't know the world? Oh, let's make fun of the older guy, is that it? Let me just say, your father is paying me a substantial amount of money to keep you from leaping off a cliff."

"From doing what?"

"You heard me."

"My father said I'm leaping off a cliff?"

"Well not directly, no." Leon is walking it back.

"So, he didn't say I'm leaping off a cliff?"

"He implied. Like the lemmings."

"Yeah, I get the analogy."

This is what happens with Leon and me. Now I am sorry Leon showed up at all. I'd rather be mugged.

I can see the Hotel Mamora from here. Its tiny square windows reflect the moonlight. The beige rounded front of the building looks more Art Deco at night than during the day.

"I'll be going now," I say to Leon and begin a quick walk toward the hotel. "Don't wait up," I call to him but I do not look back.

"How 'bout you taking the gift we discussed?"

"Good-bye, Leon."

"Hey. What about my gift?"

I wave my hand over my head but I keep walking.

"…Liora? Hey."

Nineteen

THE HOTEL MAMORA IS A thirty-room hotel that has a view of the Mediterranean and a good breeze in many of the rooms. Dalal tells me it's an older hotel that has a damp sea odor.

I'm expecting the worst but the Mamora's exterior is white colored and rounded with columns and lots of little windows. I can picture the Colonel living here. It's very French, very Art Deco. It would please his sensibilities. There is also the feeling of old Hollywood, the thirties, the early forties. I imagine Peter Lorre and Sydney Greenstreet scheming in its shadows. If Norma Desmond lived in Tangier, she would have stayed at the Mamora and slept in an enormous sleigh bed with a draping gauze mosquito netting.

The lobby is small with gray and black marble floors. It's thick sofa and chairs are a faded blood red but still have a well-kept look to them. Two young bearded men in Fez hats stand behind a mahogany check-in counter and they nod and smile to passing guests. A small high window lets a square of sunshine cut into the lobby and brighten a patch of the marble floor. An elderly gentleman is smoking a cigarette and sitting in one of the chairs. He is very thin and wears a pale blue seersucker suit and a navy-blue bow tie. His cigarette smoke curls up into the afternoon sunlight and the smoke becomes gold and dusty.

I know the room number and I do not look at the young bearded men in the Fez hats. The strap of my large leather handbag is looped about my shoulder. Folded inside the bag is the dress and shoes protected by its plastic wrap. I'm also still wearing the brown *Hijab* Dalal gave me. I like to think I look very Moroccan but I am sure that is a wish and not a fact. I probably look more like what I am, a tall skinny Jew in a tailored gray pants suit. The Colonel is on the first floor, room twelve. And I walk down the narrow hallway. A window at the end of the hall brings light and cuts the shade.

I KNOCK ON the door twice but not very loudly. A little part of me is hoping no one is home and I can get on the plane and go back to Virginia.

"…yes, yes, coming." The accent is more clipped and British than I remember.

Take your time.

I hear and feel my heartbeat and the rush from that beat goes through the sides of my neck. I want to tell myself how crazy I am and how I did not want to knock on this door, but I know that's a lie. I am constantly trying to stop the lies I tell myself and I am forever amazed at the number of them.

The door opens but only an inch or two. There is a brass chain on it. Blue eyes behind rimless glasses study me.

"Who are you?" He says and sounds lost.

"Who are you expecting?"

"…Liora?"

"If it's eight o'clock, it must be me." It's my first attempt at humor with him in twenty-nine years. When I'm nervous I will become too precious for words, my father's observation. "So do you let me in or do I eat in the hall?"

There is a phlegmy laugh and the laugh becomes a cough.

The Colonel unhooks the latch and the door opens with a full sweep. The man is in from of me. Presto, voilà. 1945 to 1974, twenty-nine years gone.

He sits in a chrome and black leather wheelchair. He is very pale, emaciated; his head leaning to the right. I gasp when I see him and I'm embarrassed by my reaction. He reminds me of the prisoners in Theresienstadt. But he still has his non-sequitur smile. He has not let go of that, my Colonel Smiley.

Tonight, he wears his tan uniform, the black polished boots, his sidearm, all the metals and the ribbons, his hat with the shiny brim. Both his shirt and pants are starched and creased. But everything looks three sizes too big. His neck is lost in the center of his collar.

"You dressed for me?" I say. He does not look strong enough to tuck in a shirt.

"My nephew helped."

A DINING TABLE has been placed in the center of the living room. Did the Colonel drag the table into the room himself or was that done by nephew Willem? Handsome Willem with the blond braid and the weathered fedora, Willem the wife beater, the one who waits for his uncle to die so he can collect. I suspect the nephew but I would not put it past the Colonel to do the dragging. He is not a man who'd let a wheelchair stop his life.

But I am wrong. Willem is placing the roasted

chicken on a linen cloth. The Band-Aid covered abrasion on my forehead begins to ache. There are two napkins and two sets of silverware on the table. Only the Colonel and I will be having dinner. I also see two white china plates with gold trim and two wood straight back chairs on either side of the table.

"Precisely eight." I hear the Colonel's voice.

"How could I miss your cooking?" I tell him.

"How delightful. Willem finds my cooking tedious. Don't you Willem?"

"Not at all, uncle." Then Willem looks at me. He has an ever-so-slight smile.

Perhaps Eloise has told him I am a person of my word. I will chat it up for him. I will talk about his loyalty and his deserving character. I have a feeling this nephew wouldn't mind if I shot his uncle and delivered his inheritance sooner than expected. Eloise's husband strikes me as a practical man.

Willem continues to bring in dishes from an area off from the living room. He wears a blue shirt and royal blue and turquoise tie. This is the first time I have seen him without the fedora. His hair is very blond and still braided in the back but the top is thinning and I can imagine him bald in the next five or six years.

The smell of roasting chicken and fresh bread is everywhere.

"Look at you, darling. So lovely." Colonel Kohler

rolls his wheelchair around me slowly. His head is cockeyed from the stroke and he uses his peripheral vision. But it is still like the old days. His inspection. He makes the same noise, as if he is about to clear his throat but never does. "…lovely, lovely."

"You're embarrassing me."

"It's what old men do."

It's difficult for him to speak and breathe at the same time and each breath has a phlegmy sound. He is not much more than paper and twigs. Seeing him this fragile is not easy for me. Mostly I look at either the floor or the table. Whatever his reasons, the Colonel was my protector and no one wants to see their protector turn too human, too vulnerable. I am embarrassed for him. I know the man very well. His pride will not allow him to be anything but who and what he was in the camp.

He is still looking at me. "Ahh, if I were forty…" he doesn't finish the sentence but no one ever does.

The room is as stoic as the barracks in Theresienstadt. There are no paintings, no photographs. There is no evidence of a smiling Fuhrer shaking hands with Colonel Kohler for a job well done.

Where is the war memorabilia?

No pistol or rifle or sword has been mounted on the white walls, no starched tan uniform preserved in a glass case. "What happened to your war?" I want to say. "Where did you hide it?" I imagine the

Colonel pressing a secret button after I have gone. The walls rotate to reveal tabooed nostalgia. The vacant white space is swapped for the red, white and black flag of the Third Reich. There are uniforms and pistols and wall-sized photos of executions. A newsreel of a smiling Hitler plays silently, the arm outstretched and stiff, the face nodding its approval.

Is this the war of your dreams?

The ending you preferred?

"How come you have no memorabilia?" I say to the Colonel. "You knew so many people. I can't believe you have no photographs?"

"What sort would I have?"

"...of the war, maybe," I say.

"The Fuhrer with his arm about me?"

"Something like that."

"Do you see me as foolish?"

"That's not what I meant." But it is what I mean.

"Our destiny was to love the Jews," Colonel Kohler says. He's bewildered by this. "...if only we had known." His smile never leaves him. "But then again, I have loved you all along, haven't I? Your sad Colonel and his lovely girl."

There is also the smell of menthol and camphor in the room. The odor of Bengay, that's my guess. I imagine it's what he rubs into his knees and shoulders to lessen his pain. But who knows if this is true.

His slender fingers move across the top of his balding head to smooth what hair remains. It is his vanity gesture, as if he is tidying up for me. It is his attempt to rise above his mortality, his infirmities, what his age has stolen from him.

I REMEMBER THE evening after dinner in his office. He had given me his sidearm. I felt his hand lift my hand and the pistol in it to his forehead.

"Go on," he had said to me. "Pull the trigger. That's what you want, isn't it? To shoot the bad soldier? Go on. I am weary of this life." He'd cocked the pistol for me but I could not do it. "Go on, go on," he whispered.

The weapon dropped from my hand.

I have thought of the lives I might have saved by doing what he wanted me to do but I could not kill him. He was being amusing, I think, his idea of amusing. He'd been a dark comic looking for a dark audience and if there was a joke to get I did not get it. A thirteen-year-old can be dramatic but being dark requires irony, a grasp of what there is to lose and what has been lost. I knew nothing then. I am forty-two now and irony is less of a stranger.

Perhaps I am here for a second chance. Is that how I take back my life? Another offering of his sidearm, is this the last supper I'm hoping we will do, first feed me roasted chicken then help me pull the trigger?

THE LIVING ROOM has candles on the mahogany end tables. A breeze goes through the two open windows. The breeze is cool and damp and quivers the lights. It has the smell of the ocean and the pines. People can be heard talking in the market below us, the narrow streets, mainly English and French, some Arabic.

"Do you have vodka?" I ask him.

His laugh is wet and ends in a cough. The Colonel guides the wheelchair towards a narrow cabinet next to the sofa. The cabinet is his bar and I watch him pour vodka and a bit of vermouth into a martini glass.

"...olive?" he says.

"Please."

"Here you are, darling." The Colonel parks his wheelchair near me. He extends his hand and the drink.

"I do love a martini, thank you." I lift the glass to toast him.

The vodka burns the back of my throat. I start

to relax right away and I know my evening with him will be far better off thanks to the drink.

Willem comes into the room again. He carries silver bowls on a silver tray. There are peas and mashed potatoes. There are dinner rolls. Steam is rising off all of it. Willem has yet to acknowledge my presence, not a nod, not even a look.

Once again, I think of the Colonel as a wall between me and whatever would hurt me. He has more strength in his hands and arms than I'd thought. It is amazing how fast he can turn and move the wheelchair alongside me. I underestimate him but I have done that many times.

"May I ask a personal question?" he says. His head remains tilted. He is looking at me with his peripheral vision, the smile forever present.

"Ask what you want," I tell him. I take my second long sip of the martini. I feel my arms and legs go soft. I am sitting on the sofa beside the mahogany end table and the flickering candle, my leather handbag beside me. I grasp the martini with both hands and balance the glass on my knees. "We all have our questions," I say. "I certainly have mine"

"What do you do? Your job?"

"I teach anthropology."

"You do? Imagine that, how fascinating."

His prejudices were validated by anthropologists who supported the Nazis and gave them the junk science they needed to argue one point or another. There are no records to show how many of these German anthropologists refused to go along with the government or how many of them ended up in the killing camps. For a while the Nazis were in love with anthropology and liked to praise them for their insights into culture and race.

"Are you married? Is there a man in your life?"

"Nothing like that, no."

"How sad. Someone so beautiful."

"I'm always here and there," I say. I feel myself heading toward all the excuses I give for not sharing my life with anyone. "There's traveling and field work. A person has to have time to develop a relationship. Dinners, a movie, whatever people do. But I spend half my time in the jungles of South America. What man is going to traipse through the Amazon with me? Why would anyone do that?"

"Another anthropologist perhaps. A man with similar interest."

"The illusive man with similar interests?"

"I would find the Amazon very intriguing," he says.

"You are in the minority."

"Did you ever...care for me?"

"...w-what?"

"I'm sure this isn't a surprise," the Colonel says. "Or maybe it's a surprise that I mention it out loud. But I was so madly in love with you, darling." He does not appear embarrassed by saying this, nor is he embarrassed by the feeling I hear in his voice. "I am still in love with you," the Colonel says. "Do not worry. Old men don't expect love. I smell too much like death now. But did you? Care for me. Did you ever care?"

"I was a child."

"Yes well. The heart is blind, isn't it?"

At thirteen, I would not have known what to say to such a declaration. But I do not know what to say at forty-two, either. It's too strange and too emotional for me. I am not given to that sort of thing. But I was attracted to him, I admit to it. But he was very evil and I despised the evil things. Many times, I was horrified and many times I vowed not to see him again.

But I also felt safe.

When I walked into the ocher colored building that was his office, no one could hurt me. He was a force I needed and a force that scared me and protected me. Who cared if the prisoners called my family Nazi lovers? They would have traded places with us in a heartbeat.

"Oh please, please," I imagined them saying, "Let us be Nazi lovers, too. Let us love the Nazis and give their little cheeks a pinch. Let us try to understand their side of the issues. Are we people who have no empathy? We who have suffered so much?

We have bunches of empathy. Look around you, this camp. Look at the rabbis and the doctors and the scholars, the educated men and women. We can grasp the sorrows of others. This is our calling. We recognize the desperation that brings people down extreme paths. Let us try to understand our enemies."

You don't think so?

How naïve, if you don't.

"I knew you were in love with me," I say.

"And you, darling?" The Colonel watched my face with his stiff bent head, his peripheral vision. He studied me the way a parrot eyes a toy. "How did you feel toward your Colonel?"

"…safe. I felt safe."

"I suppose that will do."

"I'm sorry."

"No, no," the Colonel says. "That's fine. That's what is true." He rolls his wheelchair to the open window and tries to look out into the night but the odd and frozen angle of his head will not cooperate. "I protected you and your family from more than you know," the Colonel says. He does not turn his chair to look at me. "I kept you from the killing centers. I did that. I kept you from the nightmare of nightmares, I alone. If I had not done that, you and your family would have been exterminated with the rest of them. You are alive today because of my love, my generosity."

"You know I am grateful."

"But not in love."

"No, not that," I say.

"Is it my physical condition, my age?"

"Neither of us is that attractive," I tell him.

"So, it's how I look?"

"I may have loved you when we were younger," I say. I am sitting on the sofa and sipping the vodka and thinking about what I had felt for him and when I had felt it. This memory comes and goes, nothing is stable. My past is like bad food. I am afraid I will taste it and get ill. Finally, I dismiss the thought and I say, "I was a child and not even a pretty child."

"Ah. Our ages."

"No," I say. "Not that, either."

"Not this, not that."

"Don't be impatient with me."

"It's a fault of mine. You're right."

The words start coming out before I can judge them. "Every time I started to love you, something terrible would happen." The martini has done its job and loosened me. Maybe I am feeling too loose. Another thing, I keep smelling the roasting chicken and my stomach is making a noise. I say to him, "That's what I remember, you could not stay good enough *long* enough."

"So, the war?" the Colonel says.

"Listen to yourself."

"It wasn't the war?"

What do I tell this man?

I SAW THE people boarding the trains for the killing centers to the east. They had left behind piles of clothes in the woods by the railroad tracks. Suits, dresses, shoes. Too many shoes. There were suitcases filled with jewelry and money and family albums. The Nazis gave my father several tailored suits, brown ones, black ones, wool and cotton suits. They gave my mother nice things, too.

Twenty to fifty thousand people died a day in the camps to the east.

The things we do.

"You are saying it wasn't the war?" Colonel Kohler is watching me. The skin on his face is transparent and very tight to the bone. There are ropey veins on his cheeks, forehead and down the neck. The jaw and cheekbones show a jagged look to his face. He is a skull with skin. His head is tilted an inch or so from his shoulder. "I am trying to make sense of your thinking, darling," he says. "If it wasn't the war, what was it?"

I'm still seated on the sofa. I start to have another sip of the vodka and I look at the glass and see my drink is empty. The vodka has left me feeling far too cavalier. I should eat before I drink.

"I'm sorry," I say. "What was the question?"

"Why you didn't love me back." Impatience has returned to his voice, his question now a statement.

I think about it but only for a second or two.

"You were an evil bastard," I say.

"...what?"

I may be less thoughtful than I think I am. Now I look at the martini glass and I do not know how I drank it all. And on an empty stomach. Just the olive is left and I toss my head back along with the glass and get that, too. It's salty and soaked in the vodka. I have always thought the olive is the best part of a martini.

"That's why I didn't love you back," I say.

"...because I was an evil bastard."

"You should have died in the war." I have not quit examining the martini glass. I am wondering why I drank so fast and how it would look to ask for more. "But I like you in the wheelchair," I say. I wipe my forefinger about the inside of the glass and touch my finger to my tongue. "You can't move your legs at all?"

"...somewhat, a little."

"Can you straighten your head?"

"...no."

"You're like bones in a uniform."

"I kept your family alive," he says.

"Why did you do that?

"…what?"

"An evil bastard like you. Why did you keep us alive?"

"I loved you."

"Oh please." I am studying the martini glass. "Could I have another vodka?" I say this to the glass. Then I look at the Colonel and I say, "What you wanted to do was fuck a thirteen-year-old."

"…no more vodka, darling."

I GET UP and steady myself. I go to the narrow cabinet beside the sofa and begin fixing myself a second martini. I am feeling more shaky than I thought but I am also feeling way too great and I take my time finding a fresh olive and pouring the vodka and the vermouth.

"No more vodka," the Colonel says.

"I heard you."

"Then why not listen, darling?"

A thought occurs: I have *not* come here to listen.

Miss Reba once told me to embrace the memories that frighten me. That was sixteen years ago now. "Find them and pull them into the present," she had said. "Yesterday looks different in the present."

The vodka helps. I have come here to talk and

to defy him. I have come here to leave him. I am not very strong or very good at this and I do not think I will ever be very strong. But the vodka helps me pretend. It will help me do what I want and need to do.

I am here to see yesterday and to end it.

"Remember our target practice?" I say.

I taste the martini, a tiny sip. It's stronger than the first one but that is not a bad thing and the warmth at the back of my throat feels too-too good and I have another sip to make sure the first one was not an accident.

"You're being very naughty tonight," the Colonel says.

"Well you'll have to spank me."

"Put the drink down, darling."

Willem has stepped behind Colonel Kohler. He also says to put my drink down and begins walking toward me. The Colonel shifts his wheelchair and I see his right leg extend straight out. It is a difficult for the Colonel, the leg lifting up slowly, trembling. Willem does not see this soon enough and he catches the leg at the shins and goes down.

"This is not your business, nephew."

"I wanted to help, uncle."

"That's not what you want," the Colonel says. He has his black boot on Willem's chest. The leg is weak and there are tiny spasms. But Willem does not remove the leg and he does not ask to get free.

The Colonel looks at me and says, "What my dear nephew wants is my money from the war. Don't you, Willem?" The toe of the boot taps at the young man's chin. "Gold fillings, loose change, leftovers from our new arrivals. You want what I took from Theresienstadt. That's how you endure me."

"Not true, Uncle."

"It's too true," the Colonel says and waves him away.

"Your welfare concerns me."

"My money concerns you."

Willem gets himself up and for a moment he has no expression. Then he gives me that ever-so-slight smile – very quick, here and gone. He goes toward the dark wood door and is gone without looking at either of us.

"WE WERE DISCUSSING target practice," I say. I am at the bar cabinet, looking at the Colonel, the strap of my black leather handbag still hooked over my shoulder. I will not let him sidetrack me. No brooding about Nephew Willem, not tonight. "How good is your memory? I've always had trouble with this one."

"...the drink, please."

"You placed your hand over mine to help me

aim the pistol." I am standing in front of him now, no more than a foot or so. I can smell his cologne. It's something sweet and spearminty. "I thought we were going to shoot the target in your office. But that night you guided my hand to the window and the barracks next door." I stop speaking. My eyes are hot now and I think my chest is about to crack. I remember the Colonel's manicured forefinger over mine, pressing my finger against the trigger. "Does this ring a bell?" I say but I do not wait for an answer. I do not want to hear his voice. "Two people fall, a woman and a man. The woman simply falls. But the man, he's different. The bullet goes through his head. I didn't actually see the bullet, of course. But I saw the blood and the bits of his brain leave him. Do I have it right? Is any of this familiar?"

"Put down the drink."

"I'm asking a question," I say.

"Put down the drink, please."

"Do you remember?"

"…no."

"My God."

THE COLONEL HAS grasped the chrome and leather armrests of his wheelchair. He is pressing down on the armrests and lifting his lower body. My first thought is to tell him not to do that. I want to help him back into the chair. But instead I watch him. There is a struggle in his face, the bright redness of his skin, the way the veins become hard in his neck and on his forehead. And his smile. The smile is stiff and refuses to quit.

"What are you doing?" I say. But I know what he is doing. I am not the girl who listens anymore, the child who entertained him with her bravado. I am the woman who is talking. With the help of vodka and anything else I can find. But talking. And he will never be ready to listen. But him listening isn't the point, is it? "What are you doing?" I say again.

"Put...down..."

"You'll hurt yourself," I say.

"...the drink."

"Sit down. Please."

The Colonel has wobbled himself to attention. His left hand grips the wheelchair. Then he swings at me with his other hand. What I am watching are the fingernails. It's strange what catches the attention. His nails are long and gray and he has not cleaned them for a while. He is aiming for my martini glass. It's an enormous effort, his whole body behind the swing, but I step away and he misses. And when he misses his body follows the motion of his arm and he goes down and hits the dark wood floor. I hear his shoulder snap. I do not know if it is a bone or a joint but I hear the snap and I hear a cry.

❖ ❖ ❖

"…HELP ME."

"Not tonight," I say.

"You will help me now!" This is the tone the Colonel used to give orders to the guards and the prisoners. Tonight, his voice has a phlegmy sound. The side of his head is pressed to the floor. "Are you listening? Are you deaf, you stupid girl!"

Years ago, I would have helped and thought it was my duty but that was yesterday and yesterday is not tonight. I have two more sips of the martini and place the glass on the floor so he can see it.

I am there beside him. But instead of getting up, I press my knee to his chest and pin him down. I do not realize this has happened until after it's done, until the knee is on him. Until *my* knee is on him. My breathing has turned irregular and fast. The Colonel gives another cry. I've added weight and pain to that broken arm.

"Get off me!" he says.

"When I'm ready."

"…you stupid girl."

His words are not very clear but I can understand them. He calls me "stupid girl" again and I push my knee hard to his chest and his cry is loud and I know I have hurt him.

"Look at me," I say.

He has that frozen periphery vision. And I see the anger in him. My stomach begins to cramp and I cannot get my breath. I am way over my head with all of this but I don't want to quit. I have reached my event horizon and there is no longer a speed fast enough to escape it.

I take the plastic wrap that contains my lavender and crinoline dress and my patent leather shoes from my handbag, the dress and shoes he gave me when I was thirteen. I lay it all next to him, where he can see it.

"...what are you doing?" he says. "What is this?"

"You gave me this dress, these shoes."

"...help me." There is a weariness to this, an anxious voice.

"You said you'd bought this dress and these shoes for me. 'Oh, I bought them in Paris,' you said. 'Oh, I bought them especially for my darling Liora,' you said. 'It's what the rich girls are wearing this year,' that's what you told me. And I wanted that dress and those shoes more than anything in the world. I had never seen such a beautiful dress, such polished shoes."

"...my shoulder. You must help...me."

"But I've had time to think. Years to think, many years. And I think you pulled your Paris dress from the pile of clothes left by the children. The ones you sent east on the train."

"…I've broken…my shoulder."

"My mother has faith in you, by the way. Can you imagine? To this day, she has faith, takes a sort of perverse pride in it. Mama loved your gifts to me and she loved her house with the glass in the windows, that pretty, white house with the shutters. And she will still tell me the dress came from Paris."

"…if the clothes were a gift, keep them."

"What do you mean – if?"

"I can't remember everything. You shouldn't expect that of me. I'm an old man. But if I gave you these things, the dress, the shoes, then you should keep them."

"I don't want them," I say, whisper it. "I am *not* that girl, I haven't been her in a while. These things, they don't fit –"

And I stop.

I do not know what to say, nothing feels right. What good is this visit if he does not remember the dress and the shoes? What else doesn't he remember? What else has become vague or lost in the passing of days?

But didn't he send me that letter? He must remember some things.

The vodka has slowed my thinking. None of this is *for* him. How stupid of me. What good would that do? Whether he is old and close to death or young and at the start of his journey, whether he remembers or not, it doesn't matter. I am not here to rehab the Colonel, or to make him pay for crimes.

This isn't Nuremburg.

Who has enough time for that? How would I even begin such a thing? He is too weak, too set in his ways, too senile for me to get the satisfaction I think is my due.

Yesterday looks different in the present.

Willem is watching me from the doorway of the kitchen, half of him in shadow. I think he gets it, too. I see him nod to me. We want to rid ourselves of people like this, don't we? We want to chase them from our memories, our brains, our souls. Or maybe all Willem wants is the money, and he'd like the money sooner than later.

Now I understand what I have to do.

A strong camphor smell turns my vision blurry. It's the odor of a thirty-year-old dress and thirty-year-old shoes finally released from the plastic that had preserved them. The girl who'd originally owned the dress and shoes had placed them in a pile with the abandoned clothes of many children. She was probably ordered onto a train with other children and watched that pile of clothes as the train left Theresienstadt for the killing centers in the east.

This is the dress I hold with both hands now, examining the color, the way it has faded over the years.

This is a special dress, Colonel Kohler had said. *This dress was made in Paris. It's a dress rich papas buy their very beautiful and good girls.* The Colonel had smiled at the dress, admiring it, and showed his big white teeth. He held the dress up and brushed the wrinkles from it with his free hand. *Beautiful French girls dream of wearing such a dress.*

I feel the material, so fragile, so papery and stiff. When I squeeze it and open my hands, there are tiny cuts at the waist of the material and along its shoulders. I pull at the cuts, just a gentle tug, so very gentle, and bits of cloth float like dried leaves to the floor.

It's done, I feel the relief of it and take a full breath. As I leave the Colonel's apartment and shut the door behind me, tension begins fluttering away from my shoulders and chest. My legs are still unsteady, though, and I am careful, the flat of my hand sliding along the wall as I walk down the stairs.

I've waited years for this night but more than once I had quit the thought of it. I'd felt the same about being free of Theresienstadt. Nothing was going to change, I'd believed. I would be in that prison forever. I could not imagine how it would feel to walk away, to go home. But the day did come and we did go home. And this night is no different than that. This night is for the thirteen-year-old and the forty-two year old. It's for that girl and that woman to know one another, to feel how their lives cross and go on, where one stops and the other begins.

Liora, I think to myself. *I have someone I want you to meet. She has been very patient and she has waited years.* I shut my eyes and I can see that child coming out of the darkness, her dirty wool dress, the sores on her long and bony legs.

I remember her now – not everything, not the gritty little details, but I remember enough. I can tell you how she got most of her scars, her crooked ring and little fingers on her left hand. I used to look at my body and wonder what had happened to me. Oh, I knew it must have been the camp, some accident, or some purposeful attack by a guard, another prisoner; the Colonel, too. He loved me until he hurt me. I recall the flush of his skin, the spittle on my cheeks and chin from him yelling too close to my face. His slaps. His fists. His finger and thumb twisting my ear, my nose, even my tongue. The way he'd pushed me from the dinner table with the sole of his boot. I earned that little white house. I earned it with bruises and torn skin and broken bones. I kept us alive. I got us home.

TWENTY

THE SUN WAS HERE UNTIL late in the morning but the afternoon has become shadowed with clouds. A breeze is bringing cool air from the North Atlantic. I will miss that delicious ocean and pine smell. There is no better way to wake up and begin the day.

Dalal and I are having our tea on my small balcony just off the living room. The balcony has two white plastic chairs and a round wood table, nothing all that fancy. The *Villa de France* is known more for its history than its luxury. But from here we can see St. Andrew's Church and the *Rue d'Angleterre*.

"Well I'm packed," I say.

"You're leaving us?" There is concern in Dalal's voice.

"An evening flight, yes."

"I hope your business was successful."

"Let's just say my business is done."

We both sip our tea and do not talk. I am so bad at this, the good-byes. I both hated and adored the movie *Casablanca*, that We-Will-Always-Have-Paris ending. I cry every damn time and I hate it when I do.

"You're quiet today," I say.

"You finishing things took me by surprise."

"It surprised me, too."

"What will you do now?" Dalal says.

I had not thought about my life beyond finding Colonel K.P. Kohler and talking to him. Dalal's question is one for another day. Finding the Colonel was everything and it was everything for years. Decades, really. I wanted to swap the memories of a thirteen-year-old for a very different version, an updated version, a forty-two year old woman's version. I wanted 1945 to thaw and refreeze itself into 1974.

This was not about survivor's revenge. I do not believe in that, the drama of it. Revenge is the motive of children. Mother used to say, "Growing old is revenge enough." She's wiser than I will admit. My business with the Colonel had to do with saving what is left of my life. It's about me leaving the corners and the shadows of so many, many rooms.

What will you do now?

"I'll spend my afternoon with you," I tell Dalal. I touch the rim of her tea glass with my own glass. The tea has gone from hot to warm. I have a swallow then I say, "Could you go to the airport with me tonight?"

"I would like that."

"Bring Aabid, too." "…Aabid," Dalal says and her shoulders droop slightly.

"He'll be sad to see you go. I am sure he will wear his cowboy boots."

"He's very sweet."

"I would not go so far."

"Oh you know you love him."

"I do, I do," Dalal says and smiles to herself. "If I were Christian, I would call Aabid my cross. One I bear with joy."

I have met very few people I like and even fewer that I trust. But when I do meet such a person and then I find I must continue on without him or her, I never want to do it and I never know how to do it. I imagine taking this one or that one with me. "I'll pack you in my bag," I wanted to say to Miss Reba. Leaving Peru was God awful. "I'll just slip you in my pocket," I wanted to say. It is the same with Dalal.

I want to pretend we will be pals forever.

"How's your mom?" I say. Dalal's mother is still in Mohammad V hospital and last I heard she was not doing very well.

"We had a long talk yesterday." Dalal lifts the glass of hot tea to her lips, blows on it and has another sip. She wears her brown *hijab* and her sunglasses. "I hate to see Mama so ill. It scares me. Mothers are not supposed to leave us. But that is not true. It's a lie we tell ourselves. The horrible truth is, no one is with us for very long. Particularly the people we love. I told her how very much I loved her. And I said, 'Mama, I wish I could have said I loved you more. I wish I had said it every day.' It's a very helpless feeling. Nothing can be done. I am not the Lord. I cannot make people better. And I don't care if there is a heaven or not. I want the person I love to stay with me. Isn't that what we all want?"

"What did she say?"

"That I was a good daughter."

"Yes, it's true. You are also a good friend."

I'd like to believe Dalal is talking about both her mother and about us. That is my, well, self-indulgent fantasy. But the mind is like that. Listen carefully and you can hear it speaking about two things at once.

I wish Dalal would take off her sunglasses. I want to see her eyes. I want to know what she is thinking and feeling. Or at least have a better guess. But who am I to talk? I am sitting here with sunglasses covering my eyes, too. We are hiding our eyes from each other, Dalal and me. We are hiding our clues. When I think about that I take off my glasses and I lay them on the round wood table beside my tea.

"How did you feel?" I say.

"When Mama said I was a good daughter?"

"…yes."

"I cried. What else do we want to hear?"

Epilogue

DALAL, AABID, AND I HAVE said all our good-byes and Aabid actually hugged me. I think he will miss me. Certainly, I will miss both of them. It's five-twenty in the evening and I am now alone at Tangier International. The airport is also called Ibn Batouta International. The great traveler Ibn Batouta was born in the Medina in 1304. Dalal tells me he walked the world for three decades and wrote about it in his book *Rihla* or Travels. Imagine: 44 countries, 120,000 kilometers. He wrote about religions and customs and cultural mysteries. Batouta walked from Tangier to China, from the Black Sea to Oriental Africa. He wrote about us and what we do to get along with each other and what each of us does to survive in this world.

I'M SITTING IN a gray marble waiting area. I am wearing my sunglasses and I use my scarf to cover my hair. Many people are buying tickets and the evening sunshine enters through high windows and washes the floor in gold light. I feel sad about leaving Dalal and her Aabid with his pretty cowboy boots. It is new and still baffling to me how I can attach myself to people. For so long Reba had been my only friend. It is good to have Dalal and Aabid to miss.

Tangier and I are done, that is the feeling. But I have a month left on my sabbatical and I do not want to go home and I do not know where else to go. My talk to Dalal about an evening flight was not true, well not a hundred percent true. I did not want to lie to her but how do I tell someone I am leaving even though I have no destination. What sort of person packs a bag without a plan? I do have faith, though. I have learned to follow my sense of things, my itch.

I watch the people waiting in the ticket lines, tourists with baseball caps and short pants and jeans, these are the Europeans, the Americans. They have their backpacks and cameras and tan or green duffle bags. Others wear floor length *Jilbabs* and

Hafid or *Jamal* shirts. The men have lovely trimmed beards and a few of the women hide their faces. The difference in these two worlds is never more apparent than when people are waiting in line to buy a plane ticket.

I am thinking about this and looking a woman sitting across from me on a long wood bench. The sun bright marble floor separates us but she is very familiar looking. A suitcase is on the woman's lap. Her thin white arms rest on it and hold it the way a person who cannot swim will hold a life preserver, fingers buried in it. Her head is down and her shoulders are bony and slumped. Once I focus on that tangled blond hair I know this is Eloise of Eloise and Willem. The young woman's hair drapes her face. It's her wall, her separation.

Without hesitation, I walk across the marble floor and sit down beside her. I put my suitcase on the bench. The big room has a disinfectant smell, something between vanilla and lavender. The young woman refuses to look at me and I cannot see her face through all that hair.

"...Eloise?"

Her slender fingers push the hair aside and she looks at me. There is a pungent odor about her. It's the same sweaty smell I get after I jog two or three miles. I doubt if Eloise has showered or slept.

"What happened?" I say. It is a whisper.

"You were right."

"Let's see your face."

"There is no changing him."

Eloise turns to me. Tiny cuts are about her swollen and bruised eyes. She is watching the sunlight on the marble floor.

"What did he do?" I say.

"He cut me with his ring."

"You mean he hit you."

"…yes."

"And you're leaving him?"

"…yes. Let him stay with his uncle and collect his money, his inheritance. I don't care about the money the way Willem cares. Maybe it's because I've always had money. People who grow up with money know what it buys and what it doesn't buy. That's the secret of people who never worried about such things."

"Does he know you are leaving him?"

Eloise shakes her head and the hair falls about her face again.

"Willem left after the fight," she says. "It must have been close to three in the morning. He'd been drinking last night. He drinks too much." She parts her blond hair away from her face with quick sweeps of both hands. "It's the uncle. The uncle nags and upsets him. Willem is growing very tired of it. He's always getting calls from the uncle."

I tell Eloise about my meeting with Willem in the Medina and point to the small abrasion on my forehead.

"Things will only get worse with him," I say. "You should go home. Where is it? New Jersey?"

"I can't go home." Eloise releases a tiny audible stream of air. "Willem knows where I live. He won't give up. He'll come after me. I don't know if it's love or pride. But I know he won't give up."

"Where are you going then?"

She does not answer.

"…Eloise?"

"I don't know."

There are two or three seconds of silence between us. Eloise starts to sob. I am not sure what to do so I rub her back with my palm and I tell her things will be okay but I do not know if things will even be close to okay. What do I know? Eloise puts her head to my chest and an arm about my neck. It's so very sudden, so touching. She cannot stop her sobbing. I feel the wetness of the tears through my cotton shirt.

At first I have no idea what I can to do for her. Eloise is like me in many ways or how I was at that age. Her bravado does not come from her strength. It comes from her vulnerability. This is when I know I can help.

"Come with me," I say.

Eloise looks up at me through all that tangled hair.

"Why would you want that?"

"You're good company."

"But where would we go?"

"Have you ever been to Peru, dear?"

Fomite

About Fomite

A fomite is a medium capable of transmitting infectious organisms from one individual to another.

"The activity of art is based on the capacity of people to be infected by the feelings of others." Tolstoy, *What Is Art?*

Writing a review on Amazon, Good Reads, Shelfari, Library Thing, or other social media sites for readers will help the progress of independent publishing. To submit a review, go to the book page on any of the sites and follow the links for reviews. Books from independent presses rely on reader to reader communications.

For more information or to order any of our books, visit http://www.fomitepress.com/FOMITE/Our_Books.html

More Titles from Fomite...

Novels

Joshua Amses — *During This, Our Nadir*
Joshua Amses — *Raven or Crow*
Joshua Amses — *The Moment Before an Injury*
Jaysinh Birjepatel — *The Good Muslim of Jackson Heights*
Jaysinh Birjepatel — *Nothing Beside Remains*
David Brizer — *Victor Rand*
Paula Closson Buck — *Summer on the Cold War Planet*

Fomite

David Adams Cleveland — *Ashes of My Father*
Roger Coleman — *Skywreck Afternoons*
Marc Estrin — *Hyde*
Marc Estrin — *Kafka's Roach*
Marc Estrin — *Speckled Vanitie*
Zdravka Evtimova — *In the Town of Joy and Peace*
Zdravka Evtimova — *Sinfonia Bulgarica*
Daniel Forbes — *Derail This Train Wreck*
Greg Guma — *Dons of Time*
Richard Hawley — *The Three Lives of Jonathan Force*
Lamar Herrin — *Father Figure*
Ron Jacobs — *All the Sinners Saints*
Ron Jacobs — *Short Order Frame Up*
Ron Jacobs — *The Co-conspirator's Tale*
Scott Archer Jones — *A Rising Tide of People Swept Away*
Michael Horner — *Damage Control*
Maggie Kast — *A Free Unsullied Land*
Darrell Kastin — *Shadowboxing with Bukowski*
Coleen Kearon — *Feminist on Fire*
Coleen Kearon — *#triggerwarning*
Jan Englis Leary — *Thicker Than Blood*
Diane Lefer — *Confessions of a Carnivore*
Rob Lenihan — *Born Speaking Lies*
Colin Mitchell — *Roadman*
Ilan Mochari — *Zinsky the Obscure*
Gregory Papadoyiannis — *The Baby Jazz*
Andy Potok — *My Father's Keeper*
Robert Rosenberg — *Isles of the Blind*
Ron Savage — *Voyeur in Tangier*
David Schein — *The Adoption*

Fomite

Fred Skolnik — *Rafi's World*

Lynn Sloan — *Principles of Navigation*

L.E. Smith — *The Consequence of Gesture*

L.E. Smith — *Travers' Inferno*

L.E. Smith — *Untimely RIPped*

Bob Sommer — *A Great Fullness*

Tom Walker — *A Day in the Life*

Susan V. Weiss —*My God, What Have We Done?*

Peter M. Wheelwright — *As It Is On Earth*

Suzie Wizowaty — *The Return of Jason Green*

Poetry

Antonello Borra — *Alfabestiario*

Antonello Borra — *AlphaBetaBestiaro*

James Connolly — *Picking Up the Bodies*

Greg Delanty — *Loosestrife*

Mason Drukman — *Drawing on Life*

J. C. Ellefson — *Foreign Tales of Exemplum and Woe*

Anna Faktorovich — *Improvisational Arguments*

Barry Goldensohn — *Snake in the Spine, Wolf in the Heart*

Barry Goldensohn — *The Hundred Yard Dash Man*

Barry Goldensohn — *The Listener Aspires to the Condition of Music*

R. L. Green When — *You Remember Deir Yassin*

Kate Magill — *Roadworthy Creature, Roadworthy Craft*

Tony Magistrale — *Entanglements*

Sherry Olson — *Four-Way Stop*

Andreas Nolte — *Mascha: The Poems of Mascha Kaléko*

Janice Miller Potter — *Meanwell*

Joseph D. Reich — *Connecting the Dots to Shangrila*

Joseph D. Reich — *The Hole That Runs Through Utopia*

Joseph D. Reich — *The Housing Market*

Fomite

Joseph D. Reich — *The Derivation of Cowboys and Indians*
Kennet Rosen and Richard Wilson — *Gomorrah*
Fred Rosnblum — *Vietnumb*
David Schein — *My Murder and Other Local News*
Scott T. Starbuck — *Industrial O*
Scott T. Starbuck — *Hawk on Wire*
Seth Steinzor — *Among the Lost*
Seth Steinzor — *To Join the Lost*
Susan Thomas — *The Empty Notebook Interrogates Itself*
Paolo Valesio and Todd Portnowitz — *Midnight in Spoleto*
Sharon Webster — *Everyone Lives Here*
Tony Whedon — *The Tres Riches Heures*
Tony Whedon — *The Falkland Quartet*

Stories
Jay Boyer — *Flight*
Michael Cocchiarale — *Still Time*
Neil Connelly — *In the Wake of Our Vows*
Catherine Zobal Dent — *Unfinished Stories of Girls*
Zdravka Evtimova —*Carts and Other Stories*
John Michael Flynn — *Off to the Next Wherever*
Elizabeth Genovise — *Where There Are Two or More*
Andrei Guriuanu — *Body of Work*
Derek Furr — *Semitones*
Derek Furr — *Suite for Three Voices*
Zeke Jarvis — *In A Family Way*
Jan English Leary — *Skating on the Vertical and Other Stories*
Marjorie Maddox — *What She Was Saying*

Fomite

William Marquess — *Boom-shacka-lacka*
Gary Miller — *Museum of the Americas*
Jennifer Anne Moses — *Visiting Hours*
Peter Nash — *Parsimony*
Martin Ott — *Interrogations*
Jack Pulaski — *Love's Labours*
Charles Rafferty — *Saturday Night at Magellan's*
Kathryn Roberts — *Companion Plants*
Ron Savage — *What We Do For Love*
L.E. Smith — *Views Cost Extra*
Caitlin Hamilton Summie — *To Lay To Rest Our Ghosts*
Susan Thomas — *Among Angelic Orders*
Tom Walker — *Signed Confessions*
Silas Dent Zobal — *The Inconvenience of the Wings*

ODD BIRDS

Micheal Breiner — *the way none of this happened*
J. C. Ellefson — *Under the Influence: Shoutin' Out to Walt*
David Ross Gunn — *Cautionary Chronicles*
Andrei Guriuanu — *The Darkest City*
Gail Holst-Warhaft — *The Fall of Athens*
Roger Leboitz — *A Guide to the Western Slopes and the Outlying Area*
dug Nap— *Artsy Fartsy*
Delia Bell Robinson — *A Shirtwaist Story*
Peter Schumann — *Planet Kasper, Volumes One and Two*
Peter Schumann — *Bread & Sentences*
Peter Schumann — *Faust 3*
Peter Schumann — *We*

Fomite

www.ingramcontent.com/pod-product-compliance
Lightning Source LLC
Chambersburg PA
CBHW051652180726
48284CB00006B/1965